Fire and Flint

"…my sincere recommendation to anyone looking for a completely fresh story. You'll not regret picking this one up!"

—Divine Magazine

"I cannot recommend this enough. I loved it start to finish and while it had some super sweet, it was hot too. So grab your copy and enjoy!"

—Mistress Anya's Reading Nook

Heart Unheard

"This was an incredible book about learning to deal with a disability that one never expects to have to deal with."

—Gay Book Reviews

"So, if you like Andrew Grey's previous works, or are just looking for a great book involving two men who have to overcome a lot in life to get their happy-ever-after, then *Heart Unheard* might be the book for you."

—Top 2 Bottom Reviews

Taming the Beast

"I have no hesitation in recommending *Taming the Beast* to everyone who enjoys reading m/m romance stories."

—Love Bytes

"I have always liked the way Andrew Grey writes. He has a way of writing a gentle story that has a powerful message."

—Open Skye Book Reviews

More praise for
ANDREW GREY

Fire and Fog

"Andrew Grey really knows how to give his target audience what they want. Everything about this book works for me."

—Love Bytes

"It's getting harder to pick a favorite from the Carlisle Cops series. With this sixth installment, Andrew Grey combines suspense, investigative skills, and a good mix of characters."

—The Novel Approach

Never Let You Go

"…where there's a will, there's Andrew Grey and he did not disappoint with that ending."

—Jessie G Books

"I adored this second chance romance…"

—Dog-Eared Daydreams

Ebb and Flow

"One of those books you can just fall into and forget about the world for a while."

—*Divine Magazine*

"…I would recommend giving the sequel *Ebb and Flow* a try. I know I'm glad that I did."

—OptimuMM

Published by DREAMSPINNER PRESS
www.dreamspinnerpress.com

Published by DREAMSPINNER PRESS
www.dreamspinnerpress.com

ALL FOR YOU

ANDREW GREY

DREAMSPINNER PRESS

Published by

DREAMSPINNER PRESS

5032 Capital Circle SW, Suite 2, PMB# 279, Tallahassee, FL 32305-7886 USA
www.dreamspinnerpress.com

All for You
© 2018 Andrew Grey.

Cover Art
© 2018 L.C. Chase.
http://www.lcchase.com
Cover content is for illustrative purposes only and any person depicted on the cover is a model.

Trade Paperback ISBN: 978-1-64080-507-1
Digital ISBN: 978-1-64080-429-6
Mass Market Paperback ISBN: 978-1-64108-017-0
Library of Congress Control Number: 2017915876
Trade paperback published September 2018
v. 1.0

Printed in the United States of America
∞
This paper meets the requirements of
ANSI/NISO Z39.48-1992 (Permanence of Paper).

To Holly and Mike: you are family,
and I'm grateful for it every single day!

CHAPTER 1

"HOW'S THE new job?" Casey asked as Reggie Barnett, the newly appointed sheriff of Sierra Pines, California, approached his friends at Barney's.

Reggie rolled his eyes and lowered himself into the only available seat in the place with a sigh of relief. "Can't I at least get a beer before you start the Spanish Inquisition?" he asked, wiping his eyes to get the dust out, trying to take a second to let some of the huge list of issues with the department fall away for just a few hours.

"No one expects the Spanish Inquisition!" his friends parroted back in full Monty Python style.

Reggie chuckled, releasing some of the tension. He should have known seeing the guys would be good for him. They had gone to college together. Casey was now a lawyer and building a solid reputation. Vick was a hospital pharmacist. And Bobby, the smartest of them, who had graduated top of the class at Davis, was now at Berkeley finishing a master's and planning on a PhD in mathematics. Numbers simply sang to him. All four of them had roomed together junior and senior years. Reggie smiled, remembering the action that small two-bedroom apartment had seen during that time.

Bobby placed a beer in front of him, and Reggie took a long drink, then sighed.

"That bad?" Casey commented over the din of dozens of overlapping conversations and pickups in progress, as well as music that tried to give the place atmosphere—and failed. This was a bar, not a dance club, thank you very much. Eventually someone seemed to get a clue and turned off the music.

"Worse," Reggie answered. "So much worse."

"That's why you were appointed," Bobby—a beanpole-tall man with geeky glasses and a smile that would stop traffic—said,

1

gently patting him on the back. "You're the best, and that's where they needed you."

They all teased each other, but there was no hint of that in Bobby's eyes.

"What's so bad?" Casey asked, playing with his vodka and soda, twirling the glass in his fingers. He always had more energy than any of them, and it seemed to leak out in small movements all the time.

Reggie took another drink. "For starters, I have three deputies." He held up his fingers, ticking them off as he went. "One is a drunk. I haven't caught him drunk on duty, but that's just a matter of time. I have seen him staggering home after he spent all evening at a bar. The second is so new, he asks a million questions all day long. At least he might be savable. My predecessor didn't train him for anything other than to give out speeding tickets. And the third...." Reggie rolled his eyes dramatically. "He thinks he's God's gift to the department and doesn't see why he wasn't given the job of sheriff. I have a feeling he's as dirty as a pile of dog shit. No proof, just a feeling." He drained the beer, and Bobby got him another one.

"I take it you aren't driving?" Vick said over his glass of Diet Coke. He was the quietest of all of the gang and never drank. He hated the taste of alcohol, said it tasted like battery acid to him. The group paid for his drinks, and he made sure they all got home safely at the end of the evening.

"Nope. The car is in the lot and I can pick it up later. I don't need to be back until eight on Monday, so I can drive back tomorrow afternoon." Reggie took another drink. Life was good for a few hours at least.

"Awesome." Bobby swung his arm around Reggie's neck. "I'm crashing with Casey."

"You're at my place," Vick offered with a smile. "I even have a proper guest bed now so you don't have to crash on the sofa."

"My back and ass thank you," Reggie tossed back. "Sometimes I think I'm getting old."

The others groaned in unison. "Please," Bobby said in his queeniest accent. "None of us is over thirty yet, so we aren't getting old. Personally I want to enjoy my last years of twinkdom."

Reggie snorted loudly. "You are not and have never been a twink." He turned toward the door as a man in his very early twenties came in. "Now, that's a twink," he said, motioning as the guy took a few more steps, looking at everything, back practically plastered to the wall as though he were afraid someone was going to come up behind him and take his virginity any second.

"No, that's a scared little rabbit," Casey said with a grin. "Remember the first time we came to a gay bar? I think we all looked like that, only it was the four of us, so we huddled together, whispering, looking for all the world like fresh meat for the wolves. Course, we had each other, and tongues as sharp as whips."

"Still have that," Vick interjected, making a whipping motion with his hand and nearly falling off his chair. He didn't need to drink to be a klutz.

Bobby picked up Vick's glass and smelled it, wrinkling his nose. Then he tasted it and set the glass back down. "Just soda." They laughed at Vick as Reggie looked back to where the kid stood near the wall, eyes as big as saucers.

God, he remembered how that felt. The freedom of taking those first steps out into a world that might let you be who you were, but scared someone was going to see you—or worse, no one was going to say anything. Then, after a little while, the jitters gave way to more basic instincts as you hoped against hope that someone cute would stop and talk to you, because the real reason you screwed up your courage and came was to get laid.

"What's the plan to turn around the department?" Casey asked, and Reggie grunted, watching the kid. He had sandy blond hair, and even from across the room, Reggie could tell his eyes were blue, like Lake Tahoe on a sunny day. He was, in a word, magnificent, with an air of innocence around him that made him even more appealing.

"I don't think Reggie came here to talk about work," Bobby said. "Give him a chance to unwind, relax, and eye-fuck the hell out of the guy over there."

"I was not," Reggie growled as he turned back to the group.

"He is really super cute," Casey said, making to get up from his chair.

"Leave him alone. He doesn't need any of your bad lines and lawyerly smarminess sliming all over him." Reggie sent "back off" vibes to everyone at the table, and they all suddenly found their drinks very interesting. Not that he was going to do anything. That guy was too young, and Reggie wasn't looking to spend half the night taking a guy to school.

Reggie had a strict zero-tolerance, don't-shit-where-you-eat rule, so he never dated anyone in towns where he worked. No dating, no fucking, no drama, no intrigue. He'd always worked in smaller towns and had gone to either Sacramento or San Francisco when he needed some company and wanted to fuck a hot guy through the mattress. He didn't get many chances and probably wasn't going to in the future, so he wanted to make the most of the evening.

Reggie turned back to the blond, who had moved farther into the club and was sitting at one of the small drink tables. He was adorable. His chair was pressed to the wall, and he had the table positioned in front of him like a shield.

Oh, to be that young and innocent again.

"Stop looking. I don't think chicken is on your menu tonight," Casey teased.

"Definitely not." Reggie scanned the room, catching the eye of a guy his own age two tables over. He smiled, and Reggie smiled back. Nice chest, thick arms, strong—a real man.

One of the servers circulating through the room stopped at the table. The room quieted for a few seconds, just enough to hear the guy talking.

Fantasies were like bubbles, and it was so easy to see a guy and immediately build an image of what he was like. Reggie pictured this guy as a lumberjack kind of dude. He had the plaid shirt that he damn near busted out of, and the deep tan of someone who worked outdoors. But that bubble popped as soon as he opened his mouth and asked for a martini in a near-falsetto voice. Instantly the attraction was gone. "See Tarzan, hear Jane" was a sure sign that the guy spent his days at the gym and his evenings trying to figure out which steroids to take to get bigger calves. No thank you.

Reggie turned away, took another drink of beer, and snagged a sausage pretzel snack-bite thing that a server had just delivered to the table. Food was a good idea, and he popped one into his mouth and grabbed another just as Vick excused himself and headed to the bathroom.

"Don't be gone too long or we'll know what you've been doing," Casey teased. It was an old joke, and Vick flashed Casey the bird before continuing back.

"Uh-oh," Bobby said, and Reggie looked at him. He tilted his head toward the wall, and Reggie turned. The kid still sat at his table, but now there were two other guys there, one on either side of him. They were big, tough, and had the kid hemmed in. It was a classic intimidation tactic, and the kid's eyes were like a deer caught in headlights. He stood, probably trying to get away, and one of the men put a hand on his shoulder. Another tactic. The kid sat down, eyes now filling with fear.

"The evil trolls are out tonight," Casey commented. "Why can't assholes like that leave everyone alone? For Christ's sake. All they're going to do is end up scaring the kid right back into his closet, and it'll take years before he has the courage to take another step."

Reggie understood that. He slid off his chair. He hated bullies and wasn't going to let the kid get hurt.

"Reggie, is that a good idea?" Bobby asked, placing a hand gently on his arm.

"Remember Asshole Art?" Reggie asked.

Bobby pulled his hand away, his eyes growing storm-cloud dark, and he nodded. "Go get 'em."

Reggie drew himself to his full height and strode over to the table as though he owned the place. "Is there a problem here?" He addressed his question to the scared rabbit kid, who was holding the edge of the table like it was a life preserver. "Are they bothering you?"

"We were having a drink with him." One of the big guys stood slowly, trying to intimidate, but Reggie knew that game. "Go away if

5

you know what's good for you." The words came out of Rat Number One's yellow-toothed mouth, breath smelling like he'd just eaten dinner out of a dumpster. Reggie inhaled. Neither guy smelled like they'd had a bath in a while.

"How about you let him answer for himself?" Reggie said.

"I… they… I…," the kid stammered, gripping the table until his knuckles were white, fear ramping up even more.

"I see." Reggie turned to Rat One and Rat Two. "I suggest you two get lost… now!" He reached into his pocket and flashed his badge quickly, not giving them a chance to really see it. "You have ten seconds to get up and get out, or I'll call some friends and we'll check out your cars. See what you're hiding. Scum like you are always hiding something." He smiled, and the rats stared at each other, then practically tripped over themselves to get the hell away.

"What do you want?" the young guy asked.

Reggie shook his head. "Nothing from you. I know that type well."

The guy reached for his drink, and Reggie stilled his hand. "Did they get that for you?" Reggie asked, and the guy nodded. "Throw it out. It's probably laced with something." Reggie took the glass and placed it on a tray for one of the servers to take away. "Their plan was most likely to get you under the influence, and then they'd have taken you someplace and done what they wanted and you couldn't have stopped them." He took a small step back to give the kid some room and let him know that one danger hadn't been replaced with another. "I'm Reggie."

"Willy." He swallowed hard. "Was that badge real?"

"Yes. I'm a sheriff in a small town a few hours from here. Just wanted to scare them off." Reggie patted the table gently. "I'm going to go join my friends, but you be careful. Is this your first time at a place like this?"

"Yeah." That rabbit look was back.

"Most people are really nice. Not like them. Talk to people, be friendly, and they'll talk to you, I can promise you that. Don't accept any drinks from anyone you don't know. That's just a safety issue. And take it easy and have fun. Okay?" Reggie felt sorry the kid's first experience was so frightening. He turned and went back to the table, where a plate of potato skins sat at his spot, as well as a fresh beer.

"A hero's reward," Bobby said with a grin. "That was a really nice thing to do."

Sometimes Reggie thought his sense of right and wrong was something deep in his bones. He hated injustice, and he'd seen a shit-ton of it piled on top of a crap mountain. "Thanks." He dug in and devoured the first one in three bites.

Reggie turned at a gentle tap on his shoulder. Willy stood just behind him, holding a beer glass. "Can I talk with you?"

It took Reggie a few seconds to realize what the kid meant. Then he smiled. "Sure. Pull up a stool." Reggie made quick introductions.

"This is my first time... in a place like this... and...."

Reggie nodded. "It's a gay bar. If you can't say the words, then you'll never be able to deal with the fact that you're here and that you are, in fact, gay." He pushed the plate a little closer, and Willy tentatively took one of the potato skins. He ate it almost as fast as Reggie had. Reggie chuckled. "Slow down. No one is going to take it away."

"I was too nervous to eat before I came here," Willy confessed.

"How cute," Vick quipped.

"Knock it off. Remember the first time you came to a place like this? You puked all over your own damn shoes and nearly pissed yourself, you were so scared." Reggie grinned.

"That was bad pizza and you know it!" Vick protested.

That had been his excuse for years, but they all had eaten the same thing and no one else had lost their cookies. Reggie let it go.

"Do you guys come here all the time?" Willy asked.

Bobby shook his head. "No, sweetheart. We all went to college together. I live in Berkeley. Casey and Vick are here in Sacramento, and Reggie is on the ass end of somewhere up in the Sierra foothills. We get together when we can to drink, shoot the shit, and talk about old times."

"So you aren't boyfriends?"

"No," Reggie answered. "I dated Vick for, like, three days, and Casey for a week, but we all realized we were better off as friends and that's what we've been ever since. Brothers from other mothers." He raised his glass, and they all followed along, clinked, and then drank.

"How did you…? Do your parents know?" Willy shook, and Reggie got the idea that these were his very first steps out of the prison that the closet could be.

"We're all out to our folks. We've met each other's parents."

"Casey's sister, Lila, is my best friend, and I was the man of honor at her wedding," Vick explained. "We all know everything about each other. Do you have any close friends?"

Willy nodded. "But none of them are… you know… gay."

"Well, get yourself some gay friends," Casey told him.

Reggie was glad Casey wasn't driving, because he'd already had enough to drink and was getting talkative. Vick passed over some of the food, and Casey ate a few bites.

"Don't listen to the drunk over there. You just need to take things one step at a time. It's what we all did. But we were lucky we found each other and had each other to rely on." Reggie motioned to the plate, took another snack, and offered one to Willy. Now that he wasn't looking so scared, he was even cuter than before. His eyes had lightened to an amazing sky blue, and his plump lips were red and full. He had a small nose, pert and cute, with a little bump, probably from a break at some time.

"I don't want to bother you. This is all so new." When he smiled, his straight, perfect teeth shone and his eyes sparkled. He really was handsome and sweet as all get-out. From the way he kept glancing his way, Reggie figured he had a few stars in his eyes and was maybe a bit sweet on him. It seemed a weird way to phrase it in his mind, but he felt like maybe Willy had a crush on him.

Reggie bought a round of drinks, with Willy having a soda along with Vick. They talked for a while, time slipping away really quickly, and soon it was midnight and Reggie's day was catching up with him in a huge way.

"I think…," he began, standing, "I'll be right back." Reggie headed to the restroom and did his business, paying little attention to what was going on in the stalls. If this had been his beat, he would have broken them up and told them to move on, but it wasn't his problem or his establishment. When he returned, the guys were getting ready to go, and Willy had stood as well.

Willy seemed to be waiting for him and followed him outside. "Umm…. Reggie?" Willy said, and Reggie stopped, taking a step back to where Willy stood next to the door, shifting his weight from foot to foot, nervous energy washing off him. "Do you maybe want to go somewhere?"

Reggie closed his eyes for a second, thinking back to when he'd been that young—scared, horny, and inexperienced. There had been times when he'd thought he'd die if he didn't get laid. When he opened them again, Willy raised his gaze, eyes a swirl of desire and nerves. The guy was as cute as a button, and it would be so easy to tell Vick to go on. He could take Willy to a hotel room and see what he had under those ill-fitting clothes. He could easily imagine a lithe, tight body, smooth and sleek, pretty. He needed to stop those thoughts or he was going to be showing Willy just what he was asking for, as his pants drew tighter.

"I'd love to," Reggie said, and Willy smiled. "But is that what you really want? This is your first time, right?"

Willy bit his lower lip and nodded. "I mean, I… once." He made a gesture with his hand.

"You don't want your first time to be with someone you just met a few hours ago at a bar, and it certainly shouldn't take place in a cheap hotel." Reggie wished someone had talked to him this way when he was young and stupid. "Go out, find some friends, and meet some people. Date, get to know guys, and then decide who you want to be your first. Someone who will take the time to make sure it's as special and caring as it can possibly be. You only get one first time, so don't waste it with a guy who's had too much to drink or someone you hardly know." He patted Willy's shoulder. "I know you may think I'm being preachy and stuff, but I speak from experience. You've taken a huge step out of the closet and toward finding out who you are. Now find someone who can help you take the next step on that journey… and help make it happy. Someone you care about and who cares about you. Okay?"

Reggie wouldn't have been surprised if Willy had told him to fuck off. Yeah, he'd probably come across as self-righteous as hell, but his mouth had lost some of its censorship ability.

Willy kicked at the ground, slightly slouched, refusing to look up. "Okay, I guess. But there is no one…." He seemed so lost.

"There will be. Don't make the same mistakes I did and rush into it. I got hurt pretty bad." Why Reggie was going into this with someone he barely knew was more than he could understand. The guys knew the truth about what had happened to him and that was all. Not even his parents knew all the details. "Not that I would hurt you, but you don't know me at all. You deserve more than that." With what he hoped was an encouraging smile, Reggie turned away and headed to Vick's car. The other two were in the back seat, so he folded his large frame into the front of the small car, buckled up, and closed his eyes.

"Struck out?" Casey teased.

"No. He wanted to. But… I backed away."

Casey groaned and Bobby snickered. Vick was the only one who said nothing, backing out of the space and getting on the road to the freeway.

"Why not? You would have been good to him. Right?"

"Of course I would have," Reggie growled. "But he was so scared, and this was his first time venturing out anywhere. I told him to wait and make his first time special with someone he cared about." He turned to the back seat, where the other two sat, looking at each other. "Do you remember your first time?" he asked both of them. "Was it special or something fumbling and ridiculous?" He already knew the answer because they'd shared their first-time stories years ago.

"But you would have made it special for him, and now some other guy is going to come along and probably be a dick to him, big-time," Bobby piped up.

"Shut up," Vick said. "You're being an ass, and Reggie was being nice and did the right thing. Half the people in that bar kept looking at that kid like he was a piece of meat." Vick patted Reggie's leg gently. "I'm proud of you. Yeah, you could have gotten laid, but you took the gentlemanly way and not only helped the kid, but maybe gave him something to think about. That was pretty cool."

"Yeah. Reggie was nice. The perfect hero. So as a reward, he's going home with his right hand instead of that tight, hot little body that could be wrapped around him like a pretzel right about now. Oww!" Casey groused when Bobby smacked him on the shoulder. "What are you hitting me for?"

"You're being an ass," Bobby told him. "Now stop it." He patted Reggie's shoulder. "You're right. You were nice to him. It would have been nice to have had someone older to help us when we were trying to figure shit out. Because, man, did we manage to fuck things up bad so many times. It's a miracle we didn't all die of broken hearts and end up with permanent appointments at the clap clinic."

Yeah, Reggie knew he'd done the right thing, but still, Casey was right, and it bugged him that his mind flashed images of just what he might have missed.

CHAPTER 2

"I DIDN'T see you in church yesterday," Sam Glade said as Reggie passed his desk to get to his office.

"I was out of town." Besides, Reggie hadn't set foot inside a church in at least a decade and he had no intention of starting now.

"Reverend Gabriel was asking where you were," Sam pressed, and Reggie held his breath. Sam always smelled a little like booze, and it made Reggie wary. He'd never seen him drink on the job and didn't smell it on his breath this time, but it was always there, lurking around the edges of Reggie's senses, like it came through his pores. "I told him you probably needed to be welcomed to the community." Sam rolled his chair the short distance to Reggie's open office door. "He said he'd stop by to see you."

Just what he needed—ministers coming into the station to try to save his eternal soul. "Please give him a message and tell him that he needn't bother. I am fine as I am and have plenty of work that will keep me very busy going forward." Reggie stepped behind his desk and sat, meeting Sam's gaze. "Don't you have work to do?" he asked pointedly.

"Nothing more important than God's work," Sam countered.

Reggie stood and walked over to him, glaring. The entire department was lax and did as little as possible. He had to put his foot down. "The people of Sierra Pines pay us to keep them safe. This is a place of business, and ours is law enforcement. Period. If you don't have anything to do, I will find something for you." He leaned closer. "And if you would really rather minister to my soul than work, then I suggest you head on to divinity school, and I will bring in a deputy who's interested in doing his job."

"Sheriff... I—"

"I suggest you hop to it, now!" he growled, and Sam went back to his desk. "And smarten up that uniform before you leave." Reggie was quickly coming to the conclusion that one of the deputies was going to need to be fired just to get the message across that he meant business, and he had two prime candidates. "Marie," he called, motioning from across the room to the department admin.

She hurried over, and they went into his office.

"I need you to do a few things for me. Please look up the department dress code, as well as standards of dress for the state, and make sure each deputy gets a copy, today. I will be enforcing those standards starting tomorrow." His department was not going to continue to look like a ragtag bunch of country hicks playing police officers.

"Yes, Sheriff," she said with the start of a smile.

"Also, all officers and department personnel will undergo regular drug screenings." Reggie had been up all night and found the state allowed him to do that. "They will happen when I see fit, and they will be a surprise. One failure is grounds for termination." That should put the fear of God into at least one of his men.

Marie made notes. "Is there anything else?"

"Please put in there that if anyone has any questions, they can see me directly." He smiled because he wasn't angry at her. Marie was a good admin, efficient, and did her job well.

"I surely will, and I should be able to have the memos for your review before lunch."

"Perfect. Thank you. Are there any calls?"

She shook her head.

"Good, and send Jasper in when he arrives." God, Reggie hoped he could train him properly and turn him into a good deputy who could be trusted. Jasper wanted to learn. He simply hadn't been given much training and usually spent his days on one side of the main road in or out of town, watching for speeders. He deserved more than that.

"You got it," Marie said happily and left the office.

Reggie sat back down, opened his email, and went through each item to clear them before heading into the other reports and paperwork that came with the job. He had found it a mess and had to

13

initiate proper procedures and filing processes. Marie, thankfully, had gotten right on it. Things would get better… he just needed to make sure they did.

Jasper knocked on his door an hour later, and Reggie asked him to sit down. He'd had a minor complaint that had been called in, and he reviewed it with Jasper before sending him out to handle it.

"You mean, it's not traffic?"

"That's right. Go on and see what's happening. Call in if you need any help or backup. Don't hesitate. There's no shame in it."

Jasper practically raced out of the station, and Reggie went back to work until another knock broke his concentration. The door opened, and a man dressed mostly in black with a white collar stepped into the office.

"Sheriff Barnett?" he said, and Reggie stood. "Reverend Gabriel Thomas."

"It's good to meet you." Reggie shook his hand and decided to play dumb. "What can I help you with? Has there been some trouble at the church?"

"No." Reverend Gabriel seemed surprised. "I noticed you weren't in church on Sunday and…."

Reggie decided the honest approach was best. "I don't attend church. I haven't in a number of years."

"That's a real shame. May I ask why?" The reverend sat easily in the chair. He was in his early or mid fifties, if Reggie were to guess, his black hair going gray at the temples.

"I don't think so," Reggie said. He didn't want his reasons out for public consumption, and he didn't fully trust the reverend.

The reverend straightened himself in the chair. "This is a very Christian community and almost everyone attends church regularly, including the mayor and the members of the town council." He leaned forward, his expression changing very little. "I think it's always best if our community leaders set a good example for everyone. We must think of the children and the kind of image we are setting."

Reggie put his hands together on top of his desk. "I believe you're right. We should think of the example we set. And I always think it's good if people are given the right to choose what they want to do with their own time. Freedom is a wondrous virtue." He got up and turned to the flag that stood in the corner of the office. "Making sure that the laws of our community are enforced and that everyone is safe is setting an excellent example, don't you think?" Reggie stepped around the desk and leaned against it, folding his arms over his chest. He could be damned intimidating when he wanted to be, and now was one of those times.

"Like I said, the mayor and town council all attend church regularly." There was a threat in Reverend Gabriel's demeanor.

"Good for them. Keep the city leaders on the straight and narrow." Reggie smiled and leaned a little closer as the reverend swallowed.

"So, I can count on you to join them?"

Reggie thought about it. "As I said, I have my reasons and will most likely decline your offer. But I wish you well, and please do let me know if you have any troubles that require my assistance. My deputies and I will respond as quickly as we can, and I will, of course, consult you if I come across anything of a more spiritual nature." Reggie opened the office door. "It was very good to meet you and I appreciate you coming by."

Reverend Gabriel didn't seem to quite understand what had happened. He stood and stepped outside the office. "Are you sure you won't reconsider? Won't it be much easier to conduct business with the town leaders if you see them in a more informal setting on common ground?"

"We'll see. Since the previous law enforcement of this town was deemed inadequate and ineffective by the state, all of that budgeted money was withdrawn. This department doesn't report to the city council or the mayor. I was appointed by the California Department of Justice. And I will see plenty of the mayor and the council members as part of my routine business. They don't need me butting into their church time." Reggie was pretty proud of himself. He had actually gotten through the meeting without using the phrase "no way in hell." He'd had more than enough of organized religion to last two lifetimes.

15

But it didn't hurt to be nice. "Please feel free to let me know if there is anything I can help with."

The reverend stood straight and met Reggie's gaze. "And you feel free to do the same. My office and church are always open."

"That's great to know." Reggie waited while the reverend looked to his left, and a man who had been sitting on one of the benches joined him.

Willy. It was Willy from the bar. Reggie was opening his mouth to say something when the reverend turned back to him.

"Sheriff, this is my son, William."

Willy looked even more scared than he had sitting at that table between the two rats. He was pale, his eyes downcast and his right hand shaking a little. Jesus, he was Reverend Gabriel's son. Reggie was willing to bet that the reverend was not one of those new age, more enlightened men of the cloth. Somehow he didn't think Reverend Gabriel had any sort of live-and-let-live attitude about gay people.

"It's good to meet you." Reggie extended his hand, and Willy blinked, seeming to realize that his life wasn't going to come to an end.

"You too, sir." They shook hands.

"What do you do?" Reggie asked.

Reverend Gabriel cleared his throat. "William will be following in my footsteps. He and I have spoken at length regarding his future, and we have come to an understanding."

William didn't argue, but he didn't agree either.

"Have a good day, Sheriff." Father and son left the station, and Reggie turned to the others, who were all watching him with wide eyes.

"Is something wrong?" he asked the room, and they all immediately returned to their work, so Reggie went back to his office. A throat clearing nervously drew his gaze up from his desk. "Yes, Marie?"

"Umm." She now had that scared rabbit look. "I have the memos done." She handed them to him and looked outside the room. "You… I…. Well… I'm going to miss you."

Reggie narrowed his eyes. "Where am I going?"

"He… the reverend… well, he pretty much decides what happens here. People listen to him, and so do the town leaders. They'll fire you

16

if he says so." She quivered like a leaf. "And you were doing such good things here already."

"Don't worry, Marie. Nothing of the kind is going to happen. First thing, I'm very good at what I do and will build a competent and well-run sheriff department if I have to do it from the ground up. And second, I have a sister who is married to the governor's son. I can get a message to Sacramento that will be listened to within the capitol faster than the reverend can pass out communion wafers. That's part of the reason I'm here." Reggie leaned back in the chair. "I never use that connection unless I have to, which is part of the reason it's very effective when I do. So don't worry." He looked over the memos, approved them, and handed them back. "Please get them to everyone today. Thank you."

One thing was for certain—no one was going to get away with bullying him.

"I will, and there's a call that just came in." She handed him the details, and he got up and left the office, heading out to the scene of an apparent motorcycle race.

THE ROAR of engines reached his ears before he crested the hill. Two bikes raced toward him, taking up both lanes. He flipped on his lights and the bikes skidded to a stop, turned, and drove off the other way.

"Jasper," he called in. "Where are you?"

"On my way to the station. On Sierra Drive."

"Two bikes are heading your way. Block the road. I'm coming from town. They are not to get away, and have your weapon at the ready. Do not shoot unless you are in danger, but be prepared." Reggie pressed the accelerator to the floor, cresting another hill as the cyclists realized their escape route was cut off. Reggie coasted to a stop and got out of the car.

Jasper stood behind his door, his gun brandished. "Get down on the ground, now!"

Reggie was so proud of him.

"Do you know who I am?" one of the men asked as he got off the bike and lay down on the pavement. "Who *we* are?"

"Yes, I do. You're the assholes tearing up the streets and endangering everyone you come upon. Now, stay there." Reggie had no idea what they were up to, and he zip-tied their hands behind their backs, then asked for names.

Jasper cleared his throat. "That's Clay and Jamie Fullerton."

"As in Mayor Fullerton?" Reggie asked with a bit of a grin.

Jasper nodded, clearly upset.

"See. Now you'll see," the one said.

"How old are you boys?" Reggie asked, kneeling down next to the bigger of the two. The boy quieted, and Reggie grabbed the restraint, pulling his arms taut. He wasn't going to hurt him, but a little fright might do him some good.

"I'm eighteen and he's seventeen," Jamie answered.

"Good boy. Now, here's what is going to happen. Deputy Jasper is going to read you both your rights and you two are going to be loaded into the squad car. You'll be placed in a cell back at the station, and then Deputy Jasper is going to take your statements and process both of you for reckless endangerment. Then tomorrow—yes, you will spend the night in jail—you will go before a judge and we'll see what he thinks."

"But—"

"No. See, this isn't a ticket. Not only were you exceeding the speed limit by forty miles an hour, you resisted arrest and ran."

Clay shook like a leaf. Jamie, on the other hand, chuckled. The kid didn't know when to quit.

"I'll call my dad and—"

"He can do nothing. I do not work for him, and he has no influence with the sheriff's department any longer. So your dad will wait for the judge to decide what he wants to do with you, the same as anyone else, and then your dad can pay the bail."

Jasper read them their rights and put Jamie into his car while Reggie loaded Clay. After a tow truck arrived and collected the bikes, which Reggie impounded and had taken to the lot behind the station, they drove to town. Reggie didn't talk to the young man in the back, letting him stew the entire ride. Once they arrived, the boys were put in a cell just as he'd described.

"What have you done?" Shawn asked as he barreled up to Reggie once he entered the station. "The mayor's sons... really?" He placed his hands on his hips. "You really are asking for it." There was an undertone of delight in his voice.

"They were endangering themselves and others. Is this the type of thing they do often? I imagine it is, but this kind of behavior will stop. They were terrorizing people. We had complaints that they tried to run over dogs while they were out there. That sort of thing will not happen." Reggie gritted his teeth. "And I don't care whose kids they are." Reggie took a step closer. "You need to get that through your head, and you better know that I'm watching you like a hawk. You step out of line again like you just did and I will terminate you, and I don't care who your mama is. We will do our jobs to the best of our ability, and this deferential treatment to those in authority stops immediately. Now—" He checked the clock. "—you're on traffic duty for the rest of your shift. Go on out to the welcome sign on the road into town and stake it out."

"I'm your senior deputy," Shawn seethed.

"Until you act like it, you'll be given rookie duties. Now I suggest you move before I write you up." Reggie wished he knew what it was that Shawn was pulling. Reggie had been by his home, and it was some sort of minimansion outside of town. He had a good idea of their family income, and there was no way he could afford that house on a deputy's salary. Something was rotten in Denmark, and he was going to get to the bottom of it.

Reggie waited until Shawn left, then took the boys' statements with Jasper and let them make their phone call.

The fireworks came faster than he expected.

"Where are my sons?" the mayor blustered as he barged into the station. He walked up to Sam, who shook his head and turned to Reggie. "Where are they? I want to see them, and I'm taking them home." He pointed, his face red, approaching crimson.

19

"You may see them, but that is all. They are being charged with criminal vehicular recklessness and will be arraigned tomorrow. We have statements from other motorists about how they were run off the road, and from people in that area who nearly lost their dog."

"This is ridiculous!" the mayor bellowed.

Reggie crossed his arms over his chest. "Actually, it's the law."

Another man came in and identified himself as being from the Sacramento newspaper.

"You need to wait outside."

"Is it true you have it in for the mayor?" he asked, undeterred.

"Actually, it's his children who have it in for the mayor and his career. They're the ones misbehaving. Charges will be filed soon enough, and then you can report the facts." He turned to the mayor, whose cheeks were flame-red and who seemed about ready to have heart palpitations. "Take His Honor back so he can see his sons," Reggie told Jasper. "But they stay in their cells. And you"—he turned to the reporter—"may sit out in the lobby."

As he left, the reverend swooped in, with Willy in tow.

"Sheriff, I'm sure there's something we can do to help resolve this in a Christian manner without all this fuss."

What a hypocrite.

Reggie caught Willy's gaze as he rolled his eyes behind his father's back.

"I can assure you the boys will be dealt with in a proper legal manner." He shook his head. "I'm sorry, Reverend. Charges have been filed by the people who live on that road, and there is nothing I can do about it. I know these are the mayor's boys and your parishioners, but they have violated the law and put lives in danger. Now, I suggest you and the mayor either settle down before seeing the boys, or go on home. The boys will be safe and will come to no harm." He motioned to his office, followed the reverend and Willy inside, and closed the door.

"Those boys have a history of this behavior, don't they?" Reggie asked, and was pleased when the reverend nodded. At least he didn't lie. "They need to be taught a lesson, and this is going to be a harsh one. I don't expect the judge will throw the book at them, but spending a night in jail and then having to go to court will do them some good. They need to grow up and realize their actions have consequences. I'm sure personal responsibility is a very Christian virtue."

"But those boys' futures are at stake. They both play baseball, and Jamie is up for a scholarship in the fall."

Reggie shook his head. "Then they should have thought of that before putting themselves and others in danger." He leaned against the desk, crossing his arms. "What if they had harmed one of the people they forced off the road? What if someone had been seriously hurt or killed? Would we be having this conversation, or would you be out at the home of someone you know, talking them through their grief?" He shoved forward. "You and I are on the same side. I have different methods and tools than you, but I want those boys and the rest of the community to be safe and secure. And I'm sure so do you." He raised his eyebrows, waiting for a response, and received resignation instead. "Why don't you see if you can calm His Honor down and get him to go home? Nothing more will happen tonight."

The reverend nodded and walked toward the door. "Are you sure there's nothing you can do?"

Reggie nodded. Charges and complaints had been filed. It was out of his hands now.

"Ummm…," Willy said, once the reverend had stepped away.

Reggie was a little surprised he was still here, but thankful. He'd wanted to talk to him, but hadn't been sure how he was going to get the chance. Reggie checked that the reverend wasn't still outside and closed the door.

"Not many people get one over on my dad, and you did it twice." There was no smile, and Willy kept glancing at the door.

"So you're Reverend Gabriel's son." Reggie crossed his arms over his chest.

Willy rolled his eyes. "Don't do the attitude thing, okay? Everyone does that. Besides, it's a little late to try the whole badass thing after you saved me the other night. I know you're a nice guy."

21

Reggie lowered his arms. "Fine. I take it your father doesn't know about you?"

Willy shook his head. "My dad thinks he runs everything, and most of the time he's right. The mayor and council all usually do what he tells them. Everyone both loves and fears him in a way."

"What about you?" Reggie asked.

Willy did that little dance from foot to foot. It was so easy for Reggie to read him. He liked that. Most people worked really hard to hide things around him for various reasons. He intimidated a lot of people, which he used to his professional advantage whenever possible.

"My father is…. He wants me to be like him." The confidence Willy had shown earlier seemed to be gone, and that told Reggie a lot about the relationship between father and son. "Living with him has always been hard, you know? Everyone expects me to be perfect and exactly the son my father deserves. But I'm not. I'm me, and I don't want to be a clone of my dad." He glanced at the door yet again, as though expecting it to open at any second.

"Let me guess. He'd never accept that you're…," Reggie prompted.

"Gay?" Willy whispered and shook his head. "My father would…." He shivered from head to toe. "I don't know what my father would do. He used to tell us that it was better to beat the devil out of people than to coddle the weakness of the flesh."

Reggie's mouth went dry. "Did he beat you? Does he?"

"I stay out of his way." Willy turned and reached for the door. "I want to thank you for not outing me or… you know, earlier today…."

"Of course." Jesus, at least Reggie knew he'd made the right choice. "But you know you're going to have to stand up to him at some point."

"Yeah, well." Willy sighed. "You're good at getting around him—maybe you can teach me something." He glanced out the door and then rushed over, taking Reggie by surprise. He hugged him, which was a breach of all his professional conduct. Reggie hugged him in return, but only for a second, and then Willy let go and was out the door.

Reggie followed him out a few seconds later as Willy joined the reverend, helping the mayor, who glared at him.

"You—"

"Don't blame me for what your boys did," Reggie said quietly.

"They're scared…," the mayor said in a small voice. It was clear he was frightened as well. Maybe a healthy dose of fear was what they all needed.

"Nothing will happen to them tonight. They'll be safe—I can promise you that. Now go on home, and for their sakes, as well as your own, get them a lawyer. They're going to need people on their side, especially you." Reggie opened the door and held it as the small group left.

He caught Willy's eye, and dammit if heat didn't course through him, which was the worst thing possible, for himself as well as Willy. He was so young and, from the looks of things, inexperienced with life in general. Willy had probably spent all of his life here in Sierra Pines, and while it was a nice small town, it was definitely a sheltered environment, especially for the reverend's son.

As Willy passed through the door, he glanced back once again, the lost-puppy look tearing at Reggie's heartstrings. There was little he could do to help Willy, and a lot that could hurt him, which was the very last thing Reggie wanted.

CHAPTER 3

WILLY WENT right to his bedroom and closed the door. His mother had been in the kitchen, and he was grateful she'd been busy and hadn't heard him come in. His dad was occupied, so Willy had walked right home alone, thinking of the sheriff the entire way. The man made his heart beat faster just being near him, and his hands had grown so sweaty that he'd had to wipe them on his pants a few times. The sheriff in their town was gay. Willy smiled at the thought of how his dad would react to that, especially since it seemed Sheriff Barnett wasn't beholden to him or the powers that be in the town. That would frost his dad's butt to no end.

"Sweetheart," his mother said, sticking her head in the room a half hour later. "Where is your father?"

"He's ministering to the mayor. Clay and Jamie were arrested and are in jail."

She gasped, putting her hand to her mouth. "That's terrible. The poor boys."

"They were racing on their bikes and ran someone off the road. They could have hurt people." There was no love lost between Willy and Jamie. Clay was a nice enough guy when he wasn't around his brother. But Jamie was a bully of the highest order, and he could either talk or threaten his brother into just about anything. The two of them together were terror on wheels. "They're getting what's coming to them."

His brother, Ezekiel, raced into the room around his mom, leaped up, and bounced on the bed. "I losed a tooth," he said, showing Willy his altered smile and holding up the tooth. "What do I do with it?"

"I'll take it, sweetheart," his mother said, and Ezekiel handed it over.

"I didn't cry at all, Willy." He bounced once again and flopped down next to him. Willy reached around, grabbed his brother, and pulled him onto his lap, tickling him until he squirmed and giggled up a storm.

"Dinner is almost ready," his mom said before leaving.

"Are you hungry?" Willy asked, lifting Ezekiel up into the air, to more squeals. "It's time to eat. You need to wash your hands."

Ezekiel raced to the bathroom as soon as Willy set him down. He rarely walked anywhere. Ezekiel had one speed—run—and he was always happy and full of excitement. Willy wished he could be more like him.

"Ruthie," Ezekiel whined at the bathroom door. "I was here first!" He turned to Willy, who scooped him up again. "It's not fair."

"No, it isn't."

Ruthie was thirteen and had decided that she was some sort of princess and that everyone needed to get in line behind her. Willy had heard his dad talk about it, and he didn't think that was going to last much longer. His dad didn't stand for that sort of thing.

The bathroom door opened, and his sister tried to look innocent.

"You need to be nicer," Willy told her, and Ezekiel stuck his tongue out at her. "That's not really nice," Willy scolded Ezekiel gently.

"But she's mean to me." He crossed his arms over his chest just like Willy had seen Reggie do more than once now.

"She's just being a little selfish." Willy set Ezekiel down, and he ran inside to wash his hands. Willy did the same, and after they dried off, he guided the others to the table.

Their father came in the back door. He silently greeted their mother and then sat down. The three kids took their places, and as soon as they were seated, his father folded his hands and offered a prayer. Then and only then did they pass the food, with every dish starting with their dad. It was an old ritual, and Willy had never thought anything of it until he'd been to school and seen how other kids acted.

"Is everything all right?" his mother asked.

All three of the children ate and remained silent unless spoken to at the table, including Ezekiel, though it was hard for him sometimes.

"It will be." His father looked up from his plate. "The new sheriff is a bit of a quandary. I think he's a good man at heart, but he's lost his path to the Lord. He says he isn't interested in the church, and that worries me. This entire community needs someone who will set a good example."

Willy bit his lip and took a bite of mashed potatoes. He knew his father meant someone he could push around the way he did everyone else. "He seems to know what he's doing, and you always said how the previous sheriff worried you with his lax ways," Willy said.

His father nodded. "I'm thinking we need to try harder."

"Or simply realize that not everyone feels the same way you do about everything." Willy knew he was inviting his father's displeasure, which came in the form of pursed lips and a glare. Willy returned his gaze to his plate, and once again thought about getting a job and a place of his own. He was twenty-two. It was time he stopped living at home and made his own way in life. More than once he'd thought of getting on a bus and simply leaving for San Francisco.

He finished eating and asked to be excused, then took his plate to the kitchen as soon as his father nodded. Willy went outside to sit on the front steps. There was a chill in the mountain air, so he went back inside, got a sweatshirt, and told his mother he was going for a walk. He needed to get out of the house and have a chance to think. Willy left before his father could get curious, and turned toward town as soon as he reached the sidewalk.

Hands shoved in his pockets, Willy really didn't care where he went as long as it was away from home for a while. He kept his head down as he tried to figure out what to do. Willy knew he was never going to measure up to what his father wanted from him.

Just before he reached the main street, a vehicle pulled up next to him, the window lowering. "Hey. You okay?" Sheriff Barnett asked from inside the white SUV.

"Sure. I guess," Willy answered with an exaggerated shrug. "Just thinking." A light mist collected on everything, and Willy pulled up the hood of his sweatshirt in an effort to keep warmer. "Just out for a walk to get some fresh air."

"There's a real storm coming. You should get home. We're expecting a few inches of rain tonight. Would you like me to give you a ride?"

The lock clicked, and Willy climbed inside, closed the door, and raised the window. "Thanks." Rain suddenly came down heavily. He sat still, watching the drops spatter on the windshield and then the wipers wash them away, only to have the pattern start again.

"You want to talk about it?" Reggie asked, pulling back out onto the road.

"Nothing to talk about. I'm stuck for now until I can get out of here. I need to get a job and then maybe a place of my own." Willy sighed. "This town...."

"It's a good place," Reggie said, glancing at him.

"No. It's a prison, and my dad is the warden." It was the first time he had ever talked about family business with anyone. His mom and dad, him, Ruthie, Ezekiel—they all put on this perfect face for the rest of the world. His parents were particularly good at it. "He decides everything that happens at home, and now he wants to decide the rest of my life for me. He signed me up to go to divinity school so I could help minister to his congregation." Willy yanked at the seat belt as the car suddenly felt too confining. He had to get out... now.

As soon as the car had pulled over, Willy stumbled out to the side of the road, ignoring the rain as he lost his dinner, stomach rebelling against him. He straightened up, wiped his mouth on the back of his hand, and spat to get some of the taste out of his mouth.

Reggie patted his back and then helped him into the car. "Do you want me to take you—"

"Anywhere but home. I can't go back there." Willy sighed as Reggie closed the door. He fastened the seat belt once more, and Reggie got in the car and started the engine. Without saying anything more, he drove. Willy didn't know where, but that hardly mattered as long as it wasn't back to that house.

"Where are we?" Willy asked ten minutes later when they pulled into the drive of a low log home surrounded by straight pines.

"This is my home," Reggie said. "It used to be my uncle Harry's. He died a few years ago and left it to me. I used to come to Sierra Pines when I was a kid to visit for a week or so in the summer. I came up here on vacation after he died, so when I was offered the job in town, I took it and moved here permanently." He pulled to a stop, and Willy got out. The rain had stopped, at least for a little while, and Willy looked at the porch, which filled in the front between the two wings.

"It's beautiful." He continued taking it in as Reggie unlocked the door and switched on the lights.

"Come inside," Reggie said as the rain started again.

Willy hurried up on the porch and then into the house. The inside was even more spectacular, with log walls everywhere, pine ceilings, and a huge stone fireplace from floor to vaulted ceiling. Heavy, masculine leather furniture with a few throws filled the room, and a huge painting of the mountains hung over the fireplace. Willy wasn't sure where to look first.

"Uncle Harry built it himself. It took him almost five years to get everything done, but it was all him, and it shows in every detail." Reggie took off his coat and offered to take Willy's to the laundry room to dry.

"Thanks."

"You'd better call your mom and dad to let them know where you are. They'll be worried, and they'll probably look for you."

Willy knew that was true. Heaven forbid he should have a few hours away from them, out from under his father's thumb. The other day when he'd gone to Sacramento, he'd had to say he was vising friends down there from school, and even then his dad had balked at giving him permission to go. He was twenty-two, and his dad still had to approve everything he did. It sucked. But he pulled out his phone and sent his dad a text saying he was at a friend's and was fine. He eventually got a response when his dad phoned, and after evading his dad's questions about where he was, he ended the call. It felt good to be free for a little while.

"Is your stomach settled?" Reggie brought him a glass of soda and motioned to the sofa.

Willy took the offered seat. "It will. I'm not hungry or anything." His cheeks heated from behind the glass as he sipped. Reggie had seen him throw up because he didn't want to be at home. How embarrassing could he get?

"I'll bring some crackers. It will help get the taste out." Reggie fussed in the kitchen and brought in a dish of butter crackers, setting it on the coffee table before sitting in the nearest huge leather chair.

Willy nibbled one and sipped the soda. They stared at each other, and Willy wasn't sure what he should say. "I'm sorry," he said as Reggie opened his mouth.

"You have nothing to be sorry for."

"Yes, I do. I dumped a whole bunch of family stuff on you, and my dad would have a cow if he knew. He's all about us setting an example, and we're supposed to be this model family. In church, Mom plays the organ and teaches Sunday school. Now I teach it as well. Whenever Dad wants to talk about virtue, he makes us all come forward and stand with him." Willy set his glass down. He'd been gripping it so tightly that he was afraid he was going to break it.

"Does he yell?"

"Dad? Never. I have never heard him raise his voice ever." Willy stood and turned around, raising his shirt. "Dad prefers the belt. 'Spare the rod and spoil the child.'"

Reggie gasped, and Willy knew he was seeing the scars.

"What in the hell?" Reggie asked as Willy turned back around.

"A year ago, Ezekiel was playing with the neighbor boy. Apparently they disagreed over something and Ezekiel said the F-word at the kid. He ran home and told his mom, who called my dad. Dad had gotten the belt to punish Ezekiel. I told my dad no, that if he hit Ezekiel, I'd call the child abuse hotline. Dad's eyes got black and he turned on me. I was sore for days. I was lucky there wasn't too much bleeding, but it hurt to move."

"What about your mom?"

"She does what he says." Willy closed his eyes and did his best to settle his stomach. "He's never hit Ezekiel and Ruthie. I told him he could beat me, but if he ever hit either of the kids, I would make sure he paid for it. That's when he got even more watchful. The worst thing on earth is someone who can think for themselves."

"Has he hit you since?"

"No. The last sheriff was in my dad's pocket, but I thought I'd call the state police and report it. At least someone other than that idiot would know. He's never touched me again. Like all bullies, he can't take people standing up to him." Not that there was anything he could do about what had happened now. The only thing that made him happy was that his brother and sister wouldn't be hit the way he had. At least he'd managed that.

"I'm sorry. I wish I'd been here…."

"It doesn't matter. No one can stand up to my father. Everyone in town thinks he's perfect, and they all come to him for guidance. If I told anyone else what happened, they wouldn't believe me."

"I believe you," Reggie said. "And you tell me if he abuses you or anyone in his care. I will take action." He set his glass on the table. "No one is above the law. Not the mayor or his kids. I know they've pretty much terrorized the town, but that ends now. And from what I've heard, it isn't likely the mayor will be returning to office."

"That's good," Willy said. "He needs to go. Maybe next time they'll vote someone in who isn't tied to my dad."

"You really hate him," Reggie commented. It wasn't even a question.

"I didn't always. He used to be a good man, caring. He preached the good parts of the Bible, love thy neighbor. And then my brother Isaac, he was a year younger than me, was killed by a drunk driver. Dad had loaned him the car, and the guy ran him off the road coming down the mountain. The car flew off the road and ended up hundreds of feet below. There was nothing left of him or the car. After that, I think Dad figured he must have done something wrong to deserve that kind of punishment." Willy wiped his eyes. "Mom and Dad used to be happy before then. I remember them laughing, and we went on outings, like a normal family. Since then I can't remember my father really smiling." Willy closed his eyes and tried to clear his head.

"That can change a person. I've known people who drank and turned to drugs—anything to dull the pain. It sounds like your dad turned to the Bible and managed to turn the pain inward and onto itself." Reggie grabbed his glass and emptied it. "I'm really sorry about your brother."

"No one ever talks about him at home." Willy suddenly found he needed to. "Father packed away most of his things, and no one talks about him. Ruthie asks about him sometimes, but only when Mom and Dad aren't around. Ezekiel is young enough that he barely remembers him at all."

Reggie got up and crossed to sit next to him on the sofa. "I see a lot of tragedies in my job. At least I used to. I came here to try to prevent them as much as possible." Reggie slid his fingers across Willy's, sending a shock through him that Willy didn't fully understand. "What was Isaac like?"

Willy chuckled, drawing an image of his brother to mind. "He was the wild child of all of us, though not nearly as wild as Clay and Jamie. He liked to have fun and didn't listen to our father. He used to sneak out of his room at night and go down to the diner a few blocks away. He didn't do bad things—I think he just wanted his freedom." Willy could certainly understand that. "Isaac loved cars and worked on them all the time. He kept the old family car running for a full year before it completely gave out. He was gifted that way." Willy sighed. "I miss him a lot."

Willy closed his eyes and wished he was back in his room alone so he could bury his face in his pillow and cry. He'd thought of Isaac less and less over time, and guilt raised its ugly head. With his parents never talking about Isaac, it was up to him to try to keep the memory of his brother alive.

Reggie put an arm around him and tugged him closer. "It's okay."

Willy shook his head and pulled away.

Reggie took his arm back. "There is nothing wrong with hurting over someone you lost, and there is no weakness in being comforted."

Willy leaned closer and put his arms around Reggie's middle. He wasn't sure what it would feel like to hold another guy, but as he held tighter and Reggie's arm cradled his shoulders, he relaxed and closed his eyes once again, burying his face in Reggie's shirt. He was determined not to cry, but he didn't move an inch in case Reggie changed his mind. Willy tried to remember the last time he'd been held for comfort and warmth… and couldn't. He hugged Ruthie and Ezekiel as much as he could, wanting them to know closeness and gentleness rather than the cool distance that was their parents.

He lifted his gaze upward. Reggie's deep, darkened eyes met his in return. Warm fingers touched under his chin, holding him still, ripples of heat running through him. For a second he thought he might have a fever. Then Reggie slowly moved closer.

The first touch of another man's lips to his felt like coming home. Willy hadn't known what it would be like, but it felt wonderful. Reggie's lips were hot, and smoother and softer than he'd expected.

The kiss didn't last long. Willy blinked, pleased that Reggie stayed close, continuing to hold him. This was what he'd been hoping for that night in Sacramento. He wanted more but wasn't sure how to ask for it. Heck, he wasn't even sure what it was he wanted.

"That was nice," Willy said, just because he thought he had to say something. It was the truth, but his words seemed so inadequate. Ever since he'd figured out that he was different than most other people, he'd dreamed what it would be like to kiss another man. Willy had thought more along the lines of the physical, and the kisses in his imagination had been closer to those he got from his aunts because that was all he had to compare with. This was nothing like that. It sent chills and fire running through him at the same time.

Reggie kissed him again, and the same thing happened, only this time the kiss was deeper. Willy felt it all the way to his toes, his legs extending and his back becoming rigid, excitement coursing through him. Willy wound his arms around Reggie's neck, holding him close because he never wanted this to end.

The heat that traveled between them set Willy's world on fire, burning away the person he thought he was. This was someone different, someone who had kissed another man and knew he wanted to do it again and again for the rest of his life. When they parted,

Reggie released him, and Willy sat back on the sofa, breathing deeply, blinking, wondering how he was going to deal with the changed reality of his life.

It was just a kiss. And maybe that was true. But to Willy, it was more than that. It was assurance that what he'd thought was real and not some fantasy. He'd had a taste of what he really wanted.

"You okay? You look a little dazed," Reggie asked, and Willy nodded absently. So many of the things his father had always said about gay people were complete shit. He could see that now. Things about them being deviants and rapists, which was only a bunch of shit to scare people into believing the same narrow-minded things that he did.

"Yeah." Willy smiled. "I'm fine, more than fine. I think I'm good… for the first time in a long while." It felt like the sun had come out from behind the clouds after a long rainstorm.

Maybe things would be all right after all.

A crack of thunder split the air. That kind of storm was rare up here, and Willy jumped, not used to hearing it. They got plenty of rain and snow in the winter, but thunder didn't happen often, and that meant the storm was intensifying. Willy sat back as rain pelted the windows. "This place is solid as anything ever built." Reggie gathered him close once again. "Nothing to worry about."

Willy wasn't worried, really. Reggie was strong and protective.

After a while, the storm abated, and Reggie got up, made a snack, and brought it in. "I don't have a great deal in the house right now." He'd grabbed some meat and cheese to have with the crackers. Willy's appetite had returned, and he ate carefully, then yawned.

"I should probably go home." Though the prospect was hardly something he looked forward to. But a few hours of freedom would have to hold him for now.

Just then the wind rattled the windows, and Reggie checked his phone. "If we lose power, I'm going to have to go see what's wrong and what I can do to protect the repair crews."

"You have to go out in this?" Mountain storms could come on fast and the wind could whip through the canyons with hurricane force.

"I hope not." Reggie stood, and Willy did the same. "Let me show you the guest room. No one should be out in this who doesn't have to be." Reggie led him down a hallway and opened the door to a bedroom with the same log walls and furniture with frames made of branches. "My uncle made a lot of the furniture himself as well. He loved using materials he gathered himself." Reggie pointed out the bathroom and then left Willy alone, closing the door.

Willy sat on the edge of the bed, listening as Reggie returned to the living room. He cracked the door and the clink of dishes reached his ears. Then Reggie approached, switching lights off.

Willy went into the bathroom to clean up. He got ready for bed and settled under the covers as Reggie moved in other areas of the house. Willy wondered what it would be like to have Reggie in bed with him, the huge, strong man lying next to him, holding him close. He tried not to imagine what sex would be like with him. Basically he had so little experience, his fantasies were mundane and repetitious. He needed to get some new material and maybe some new experiences to go along with it.

A soft knock pulled Willy out of his thoughts. "Willy?"

"Yes," he answered gently, his body instantly on edge, excitement coursing through him as he wondered what Reggie wanted. What would he do if Reggie came in the room? God, Willy was too scared of his own damn shadow. Reggie was a good guy. He'd backed off at the club, and he'd certainly make sure Willy was taken care of.

"If you need anything, my room is at the end of the hall."

"Okay," Willy answered, and then Reggie was gone and he was alone, yet so close to what he thought he wanted. The thing was, he had no idea how to go about getting it. Maybe if he asked...? No, Reggie had already backed away from him once.

CHAPTER 4

REGGIE YAWNED at his desk the following morning. He hadn't slept much the night before, keenly aware of having Willy in the house. When he got up at his usual time, he'd found Willy already awake, sitting on the sofa, staring at the walls, worrying his lower lip with his teeth. He'd taken him back into town and dropped him off at home before heading to the station. Now, he couldn't concentrate, hoping Willy wasn't going to be in any trouble.

"When do we need to take Clay and Jamie to see the judge?"

Reggie checked the clock. "Go get them and we'll take them over. How was their night?"

"Very quiet. The older one, Jamie, apparently stayed up, and Clay spent much of the night on his bunk. The guard thought he might have heard crying on and off during the night, but he wasn't sure." Jasper shifted as he took another step closer. "What do you think will happen to them?"

"Honestly, I think they'll be given bail and then they'll get probation and a fine in the end, especially Clay, who's a minor. The worst part of their ordeal is probably over, but I hope they remember it." Reggie stood and went with Jasper through the station. "Where is Sam?"

"Traffic duty." Jasper grinned. It was clearly a source of delight. "Shawn is out on a domestic disturbance call up at the Wilsons'. They were screaming at each other again, and the neighbors called." He spoke like that was a regular thing. "Shawn says they never hit each other, just yell at the top of their lungs like banshees. I went out there once, talked to them. They get quiet for a while, and then it starts up again."

They got the two boys out of their cells and into the cars, and drove them to the courthouse, where they were met by their parents and a lawyer. Reggie escorted them to a secured room where they could talk and left Jasper to watch over them. He headed upstairs to the courtroom and ran into Reverend Gabriel.

"Good morning. How was His Honor doing?"

"As well as can be expected. I counseled him on his boys, and we prayed together. Then I left him alone." Reverend Gabriel held his hands together, his voice as calm as ever. Reggie wondered what was really going on behind those eyes.

"He's with his boys and the lawyer now." Reggie did his best not to look around in the hope that Willy was with his father, but the door to the men's room opened and Willy came out, dressed in somber clothes much like his father.

"Morning, Sheriff," Willy said with a slight smile that lasted seconds, before standing next to but behind his father, gaze darting around, tension between father and son mounting by the second.

"I understand you brought my son home this morning." Reverend Gabriel turned to Willy and then back to him. Reggie wondered what Willy had told him and suspected this was a way of corroborating Willy's story. Reggie nodded, and thankfully Jasper brought out the boys, so they headed into court without him having to answer.

EVERYTHING WENT as expected: bail and a court date were set, and the case shifted to the county attorney, which meant that unless it actually went to trial, Reggie and Jasper were done.

"Where is your father?" Reggie asked Willy as he approached him outside the courtroom.

"He had to go to the church, and I managed to beg off. I can only take so much of this. I was hoping to have a chance to talk to Clay." Willy peered up toward the doors. "He's at a crossroads. You know?" He gazed past Reggie and waved. Clay stood with his brother and father, still looking a little freaked.

Willy stepped away and motioned him over. Clay approached slowly, warily. It was clear he wasn't interested in spending time around the sheriff who had arrested him. "Are you going to put me in jail again?"

"Clay," Willy said gently, "the sheriff isn't to blame for what happened and you know it. He's doing his job, and what you and Jamie were doing was wrong. Whose idea was it to race?"

Clay's glance shot to Jamie and then back to Willy.

"I see. You know, you're old enough to think for yourself, and you need to start doing that."

"But Jamie—"

"Is your brother, but he gets into trouble and takes you along with him." Willy was amazing. He was kind and caring. "You're better than that. Jamie is an adult and he's going to face the music for this one, harder than you will, since you're still seventeen." Willy hugged Clay gently, and Reggie could no longer hear what they were saying.

Once they pulled apart, Willy watched as Clay went back over to his father and brother. The group moved away, and Reggie turned to Jasper.

"Go back to the station, make sure there are no calls, and then head on out for traffic, but keep your radio on. I want you to get more experience, and that means taking more calls." Reggie smiled as Jasper hurried away. He might have actually jumped a little before he reached the stairs.

"Where are you heading?" Willy asked.

"I'm going to patrol for a while. I want the department to be visible. Let people see that we're out and about, not just sitting in the station. What about you?" Reggie found it hard to look away, but he had to. Having Willy in his house had been hard as hell. Every sound had made Reggie sit up, wondering if Willy was okay. He'd tossed and turned for hours, debating if he should have offered to stay with him, to see if Willy wanted to come to his bed. He knew he'd done the right thing, but still….

"I don't know. I was thinking I could look for a job." Willy lifted his gaze, the confidence from earlier gone. "I need to be more independent."

37

"That's not a bad idea."

"How late do you work tonight?" Willy asked. "I can cook really well. So maybe…."

Reggie was on the verge of saying yes. It would be nice to have dinner with Willy, but that would be playing with fire. He never dated or got involved with guys where he worked, ever. It was a bad idea on all levels, and yet he wanted it, consequences be damned.

"You don't have to…," Willy whispered, glancing around.

"I know that. But what sort of chance will you be taking?" *Would we be taking?* "You know what will happen if your father finds out."

Willy nodded. "I know. But I need to have a little freedom of my own, a chance to be myself with someone, or I'm going to go out of my mind. I can't sit at home, nodding my head, making believe that I agree and want what my father does." Willy took a single step closer. "I'm not strong like you. I can't just stand up to him like that."

"You did before," Reggie said, wishing he'd kept his mouth shut.

"And look what it got me. Permanent souvenirs of how far he'll go to try to protect what he sees as his mission in life." Willy sighed and turned away, walking slowly toward the stairs.

"Six," Reggie said. "I get off at six, depending." His radio came to life in his ear, and he hurried to the exit on his way to a call. He didn't have time to be any more specific than that, and maybe that was okay. Now it was up to Willy to figure out what he wanted to do with the information.

REGGIE SPENT the day on one call after another. When he had a few minutes to patrol, he made a point of stopping out at the highway rest area to check on the restrooms. They were a known spot for men to meet. Not that he had anything against it, exactly, but it was also a spot where other kinds of transactions could be conducted. Since he wanted to choke those off, he'd added the area to regular patrols. But other than a family of four who were walking back to their car as he arrived, it was empty and as it should be. He drove through, taking pains to be visible to anyone passing, and then headed back toward town as he received another call.

After his last call, Reggie went to the station and got to work. He had reports he needed to file, and he reviewed those of his deputies. Sam had said that he'd seen a number of cars out at the rest area, though when he pulled in, the parking lot emptied within minutes. As Reggie read through the report carefully, things didn't ring quite true, especially some of the timing. It could have been sloppy reporting on Sam's part... or something else. He needed to keep a closer eye on him.

Sighing softly, he put the papers aside and finished up for the day, making sure all on-call information was correct. Sam was on duty that evening, so Reggie hoped for a quiet night. He checked in with him and found Sam almost chipper, which was unusual.

"I got things. You have a good night."

Reggie thanked him and left the station, heading home for a few hours of peace. He pulled up in front of his home and found it quiet. Reggie checked the time—a little after six. He drove into the garage, then walked across to the house and entered the nearly silent abode. Reggie had to admit that he was a little disappointed. In truth, he'd been looking forward to the possibility that Willy would come over. He was also well aware that carrying on a relationship with Willy was a really bad idea. But damn, as soon as he closed his eyes, he could see Willy, and if he concentrated, he could feel him in his arms, a bundle of heat and energy.

He went to his bedroom to change out of his uniform and take care of his belt and gun before returning to the kitchen.

A car pulling into the drive caught his attention, and Reggie hurried to the window, moving faster than he should have. Willy got out of an old Toyota that looked held together with duct tape and a prayer. Maybe that was an exaggeration, but it was in some serious need of attention. Reggie went right to the door and opened it so Willy wouldn't need to set down the plastic bags he was carrying.

"What's all this?" Reggie asked as Willy set the bags on the counter.

"I said I was a good cook, and I didn't know what you had." He began unpacking the bags, pulling out some tomatoes and cucumbers that looked amazing. There was leaf lettuce, and then pasta and basil, the scents filling the kitchen. "Most of this came from my garden. I have a patch in the community plot south of town, and I raise a few things, mostly for my mom."

"My uncle had a garden out back. He'd cleared some trees for it. I haven't had a chance to do anything with it. But this fall I'll till it and then plant in the spring. Not that I know all that much about growing vegetables, but I thought I'd give it a try." Reggie had the space and figured it would give him a new hobby.

"I've been growing things my whole life. I love it. You have to be careful, though, especially in this area. Only get plants from local growers or seeds that are purchased locally. They carry hardier varieties that can thrive at our altitude. And California has a bunch of agricultural laws to protect the rest of the state from invasive species." Willy blushed. It was adorable and sweet as anything. "You probably knew that."

Reggie got him a pot for the pasta and a bowl before showing Willy where everything else was. Then he got out of the way. "Where did you learn to cook?"

"Mom thought it a good idea that all of us know some of the basics." Willy began chopping the basil, the scent filling the room. "I can make garlic bread if you want...."

Reggie got out the bread, and Willy pulled some cloves of fresh garlic out of his bag. Reggie was beginning to wonder just what else he had in there.

"Mom taught me and I liked it. But I never get to cook much. Dad is pretty old-fashioned about things like that. Sometimes I think he was born too late." Willy finished with the basil and filled the pot to get the pasta on. "I didn't have the cash to get some meat, but...." Willy opened the refrigerator to check for butter. "Yes. I took a chance. I'm going to make some pesto and a salad and garlic bread. Is that okay?"

Reggie's stomach growled at the mention of food. "More than. I'm so sick of my own cooking."

"What do you make?"

Reggie humphed. "I usually get stuff I can put in the microwave and heat up. I can grill a mean steak and make good chicken and mashed potatoes. Basic stuff. But I'm usually so busy, I don't have a lot of time for things like that." He pulled out one of the stools from the living room side of the island and sat down, watching Willy as he got the pasta water on the stove and cut up everything he needed.

"This is a great kitchen. Mom's is really small. She has just enough room to do what she needs to, but if anyone else is in there with her, it gets crowded fast. This is so open and comfortable."

"I'm glad you like it." Reggie sat and watched. "Can I ask you something? Why are you doing this?"

Willy's knife stopped midslice, the blade halfway through the cucumber.

"Not that I don't appreciate it, because I really do. But why do this? Why invite the possible wrath of your father?"

Willy rolled his eyes. "We haven't done anything other than cook." He tried to look innocent but failed. "Okay...." He set the knife down. "I'm tired of my dad running my life for me, and I like you. I know you may not like me or you may think I'm too young or something." Willy rocked back and forth slightly, which told Reggie he was nervous. "You've been nice to me, and you actually see me. Do you know what that means?"

Reggie was lost for words. "No?"

"I'm Willy, the reverend's son. Most of the time, when I'm with him, people don't even see me. They all defer to him and pay attention to him. I went through high school with very few friends because I was nearly invisible. But you saw me at the club, and even here. There are people in town who think of me as Reverend Gabriel's son—that's all. I'm not Willy. I don't have my own identity. They might know my name, but they don't even think of me as my own person." Willy looked down and went back to cutting. "Maybe I'm being foolish to think that someone like you would...." He set down

41

his knife. "I am being dumb, aren't I?" He backed away from the counter. "I am being stupid. I thought I could come over here, make you dinner, and then maybe we could… I don't know." He turned and left the kitchen, striding toward the front door.

"Where are you going?" Reggie asked, jumping off his chair, desperate to relieve Willy's stress and anxiety.

"I should just leave you alone and not bother you. I'm some kid who has no clue about how things work and—"

Reggie caught Willy's arm as he reached the door. He didn't grip him hard—he'd never hurt him—but Reggie didn't want Willy to go. "Hey, I see you." When Willy turned, Reggie's heart skipped a beat at the loneliness in those crystal-blue eyes that seemed to change color with the light and with Willy's mood. They were fascinating, and Reggie wondered if he would ever be able to see all the colors they could be. "And you don't need to leave." He tugged Willy closer, wrapping him in his arms, marveling at how right he felt there.

"I shouldn't have come. You were right about my dad finding out. Me hoping for things and wishing for things… you doing this… you…. It's playing with fire."

Reggie held him tight, his heart rate increasing, a nearly overwhelming urge rising from the base of his spine, blooming like a spring flower, spreading and growing by the second. He leaned in, closing his lips over Willy's, tasting his sweetness, wanting more as soon as he'd gotten another taste. He tightened his grip, intensifying his hold, as a need to protect and care for Willy grew by the second. Reggie was in deep trouble; he could already feel it. If he'd been smart, he'd have let Willy leave. This was throwing all his rules out the window, and while he liked it, the idea threw him for a loop. He pulled back, still holding Willy, gazing into his eyes, trying to think clearly.

Clearheadedness was a lost cause. A few blinks of those blue eyes and a glimpse of Willy's pink tongue as it peeked out to wet his lips was enough to counteract everything he knew he should do.

"Let's have dinner. Okay?" Reggie asked in a whisper, not wanting to spook Willy.

Willy nodded, and Reggie walked with him back to the kitchen. As Willy took up the knife again, Reggie went into the living room and put on some music—nothing too loud, but something to fill the void and create a mood.

"I feel like a fool," Willy said without looking up from what he was doing.

"You can't assume things. If you want to know something about anything, all you need to do is ask. It's that simple." The music changed and the beat increased. Reggie tapped his foot and then spun around in time to it. Willy chuckled, and Reggie hurried around to the back of the island and set the knife on the counter before whisking Willy into his arms, dancing him out of the kitchen and into the living room.

"I need to finish this if we're going to eat," Willy said, nearly tripping over his own feet. Reggie held him up, and they moved more easily together once Willy relaxed.

"There you go. I take it you've never been dancing," Reggie said, holding Willy closer and letting the music work its way through him. "Is that something your dad doesn't allow?"

"No. He and Mom used to go dancing together sometimes. There's plenty of dancing in the Bible, so he isn't against that. But I never learned. I'm kind of uncoordinated. Mom tried to teach me once, but I ended up falling and breaking a lamp. There were no more dance lessons after that. Mom didn't want to have to replace the rest of the furniture in the house." Willy laughed, and Reggie chuckled against his neck, inhaling his deep, musky scent and letting it fill him as the song came to an end. He let Willy go, glad for a breather and maybe a little distance. Sitting on that stool was going to be difficult for a few minutes. Reggie only hoped his excitement wasn't too obvious.

"Is there anything I can do to help?"

"See what you have for salad dressing." Willy put the pasta in the boiling water and began making up the pesto, which smelled mouthwateringly good within minutes. Reggie had some honey mustard and a bottle of ranch dressing and put them on the counter. Then he helped butter the bread, and Willy put it into the oven.

43

Reggie should have made sure he had a snack of some sort other than crackers and cheese like he'd served the last night. Still, it wasn't going to be long before dinner would be ready, though the scent was driving him crazy.

Willy took out the pasta and sauced it, then placed the bowl of salad on the island, as well as the pasta, before getting the garlic bread out of the oven and tipping it onto a plate. Reggie got a couple of beers from the refrigerator to complete the feast, and they sat side by side on the stools.

"Wow, this is awesome," Reggie said around his first bite of linguini. The scent had nothing on the rich creaminess of the pesto sauce.

"I read about this in a magazine and made it for some friends when I was in college. But I never made it for my family." Willy shrugged.

"Where did you go to college?"

"I got into UC Davis, and I was there for two years. I had it good there and enjoyed it. I was Willy for that time, but budget cuts meant that my scholarship money dried up, and Dad wasn't going to help pay for it. He likes to think he runs the town, but one thing I do know, my father is honest as far as money is concerned. He doesn't take any from anyone and only pulls his salary from the church. So there isn't a whole lot to go around. After that, I came back here. How about you?"

"I'm a Davis alum as well. But I was probably there and gone before you. I majored in criminal justice." Reggie took another bite of pasta. "I started out as a sheriff's deputy in the Fresno area, where I did well and helped on some high-profile cases. I busted a huge drug distribution ring, and that got me some recognition. I was asked to take over a department that was struggling, and when I agreed, they sent me here."

"So this is your first time as sheriff? You do seem young." Willy took a bite of a piece of garlic bread, and Reggie reached for one as well.

"I was acting sheriff there after my boss was implicated in the ring I broke up." Reggie sighed. "That was the hardest thing I ever had to do. He'd taught me what I know and given me my first break, but he was dirty. That really shook me up." The decisions he'd had to make had nearly torn his soul apart. In the end, he'd done what was right, but it had ripped him apart emotionally. "I looked at the guy like a second father."

"I'm sorry." Willy placed his hand on top of Reggie's, their fingers curling together. "What about your family?"

Reggie took a bite of bread, just garlicky and gooey enough to be totally decadent. "Mom and Dad are in Sacramento. They're proud of me, and my dad was right there for me when the shit hit the fan. My sister, Janine, was ready to marshal the troops and have them there to buck me up. But I needed to work through it on my own." That was partially why he was so careful about relationships now. He had built a very close one with Sheriff Andy, and look what happened. It was best to keep professional relationships and personal ones as far apart as possible. And he'd done that… up until a certain young man with the most amazing eyes walked into his station.

"You know, I'm tired of talking about families. Mine pretty much sucks."

"Then what would you like to talk about?" Reggie was more than willing to change the subject.

"Oh!" Willy's eyes brightened and he leaned closer. "I think I got a job. John Webster down at the drugstore is looking for someone to help him with his books. The person who was helping him quit, and he's been trying to do it himself and is going crazy. I took accounting classes in college, so I can help him do that. He's happy and says that bookkeeping is a half-time job, but he can use me to watch the store and things when he's gone, so that would be the rest of the time. I'm not going to get rich or anything, but I will be able to have some money of my own."

"What did your dad say?"

"I didn't tell him yet. I talked to Mr. Webster just before I came here, but he wants me to start on Monday. So that's really good."

Willy practically bounced on the stool. "The really nice thing is that Mr. Webster is Catholic, so he isn't one of the folks who's beholden to Dad. He wants me for me and what I can do."

"That's great." Reggie smiled.

Willy bit his lower lip. "The only thing is that Mr. Webster is open on Sundays. He's about the only store that is, but he said that people need things and they come in all the time. He doesn't open till after noon, but it means that some days I'd have to leave church early. But the store is just down the street, so I can be there in five minutes. It won't be too big a deal."

"You deserve to have your own life." Reggie lifted his beer bottle and clinked it with Willy's. They shared a smile and then drank. "Sometimes fathers think they know what's best for their children. Maybe they do sometimes, but we have to find out on our own."

"Maybe once I get settled in this job, I can find a place of my own to live. That would be best. Then I'd be away from him. But I suppose I need to go one step at a time." Willy was still so excited, and Reggie was amazingly happy for him. Taking the first steps on one's own was a big deal, though it highlighted just how big the age and experience difference was between them. "How was your day after all the court stuff?"

"Busy, but relatively uneventful, thank goodness. I took some calls, mostly community-service-type things, and did some patrolling." Reggie didn't explain about the rest area and the stepped-up patrols he'd ordered there. He figured there was more going on there than just a little quick gratification.

They ate companionably. Reggie couldn't help glancing over at Willy every few minutes just to check on him. Reggie wished he'd have sat on the other side of the counter so he could watch Willy more closely. On second thought, Reggie was already doing his best to keep his napkin stretched over his lap to hide his erection. Just being this close to Willy had that effect on him. Not that he had any intention of acting on it, even though his instinct pushed him to take Willy and show him just how wonderful things could be between two people.

Reggie stifled a sigh once he was finished eating. He needed to put some distance between them. Reggie was already sweating, and not from the heat. Every time he inhaled, he scented Willy. Maybe it was his cologne, but Reggie didn't think so. He was pretty sure he kept smelling pure Willy, and it was driving him crazy.

He put his dishes in the sink and began gathering up the leftover bread and pasta to wrap it up and put it away. Between them they had eaten all of the salad, so he put that bowl in the sink.

"I appreciate you coming to make me dinner. You didn't have to, but it was a real treat." Reggie smiled and then finished the cleanup.

"I see…," Willy said softly. "I really should get going."

Reggie didn't mean to make Willy feel bad, but Willy was a huge source of temptation. Reggie turned around, pulling his hands out from under the warm water. "I don't know what you want from me," he admitted. "Or maybe I do." Fuck it all to hell, he hated being nervous. In his job, it was action, caution, and confidence that kept you on your toes and alive. Inaction could be just as fatal as making the wrong move.

"I feel like a fool," Willy whispered. "Maybe I am too… naïve for words." He rolled his eyes and looked about two seconds from slapping himself. "I figured I'd come over here and make you dinner, and we'd talk and you'd see that I'm a nice guy, maybe sort of cute…." His half smile certainly was—there was no denying that for a second. "I thought that maybe you liked me and that…." He sighed. "Ruthie hates to cook, and Mom is always telling her that the way to a man's heart is through his stomach. At least that's how she claims to have caught my father…."

"Is that what you wanted—to catch me?" Reggie was flattered and a little bowled over by the simple, old-fashioned approach. He walked to where Willy stood and embraced him gently. "You're an amazing young man. Don't let anything tell you otherwise, ever." He tightened his hug, and Willy wound his arms around Reggie's waist.

"Sometimes I wish I was like everyone else. Then I wouldn't have to hide and could be myself." Willy squeezed him. "I just want what everyone else has." He lifted his gaze, and Reggie nodded. He understood that sentiment so very clearly.

"I hide too," Reggie admitted. "When I want to have fun, I go to Sacramento. I never see anyone where I work. That's where we met, on one of those evenings. Those friends all live very open lives, but I keep mine closed. The people who appointed me to my position here do know that I'm gay." Reggie swallowed very hard. "I love my job and I love what I do. As much as I want to be able to say that my being gay doesn't make a difference, I know that's not really true. It will make a difference. And who knows how the people here will take it?"

"So you're staying away from me because of them?" Willy asked.

Reggie chuckled, burying his nose on Willy's soft hair. Without thinking, he inhaled and had to stifle a groan. "No. I'm staying away because I'm afraid you'll become addictive, and the two of us being together is dangerous. You have a pretty good idea how your father will react. Imagine what would happen if it came out that you and I are together." Reggie closed his eyes and held a little tighter because what he was saying made his throat ache and close up as though it wanted to stop what he was saying.

"I guess I know," Willy said, lifting his gaze, and when Reggie met those incredible blue eyes, they drew him in like a magnet, a force he couldn't control, until he had to stop. Willy's heated breath touched his lips, ghosting over them. Reggie froze, holding at bay the urge to take what he wanted. This was a moment of decision, and it had to be Willy's. He had to make the final move.

Their lips touched, Willy closing the distance. A frisson of electricity shot between them. Reggie tried to keep the kiss gentle, but Willy pressed closer, so he went with it. His right leg shook slightly with excitement, and Reggie slid a hand down Willy's back, along the curve, and then down to the top of one of his cheeks. Each step forward was fraught with peril as Reggie inched toward an abyss that there would be no turning back from.

Somehow he managed to break their kiss. "We need to take things slow, okay?" Reggie's heart pounded and the thumping rang in his ears. He took a deep breath and held it, hoping to give his head some time to clear from the fog of pure desire that had fallen over it. He blew out the breath he was holding.

"Yes, slow," Willy agreed and kissed him again, harder, Willy quivering in Reggie's arms. Somehow he knew he'd just been lied to, but Reggie was too far gone to care. Willy practically hung off him, making soft noises in the back of his throat, stoking Reggie's desire by the second. Reggie held him closer, groaning himself as Willy's cock pressed to his. God, he hated the layers of clothing between them, and yet they were the only things preventing him from throwing Willy over his shoulder, carrying him to the bedroom, and tossing him on the bed. His imagination raced with images of Willy naked on his bed, smiling up at him, pale skin against the burgundy coverlet.

Reggie stilled and then backed away, his arms slipping from around Willy. "Okay...." Damn, he needed a second, because what the fucking hell? Willy was better than a dose of Viagra, and Reggie needed to be able to think. His rules. Reggie needed to remember the rules. They were there for his safety and future. He wasn't supposed to be doing this.

"Okay. I take it this is the 'taking it slow' part?" Willy said, his breath coming in soft pants.

Reggie nodded. "Do you want to watch a movie or something?" He didn't want Willy to go. "I have some in there if you want to stay. You could pick one out, and I'll be right back." He needed a little distance. And a damn beer.

He got a beer and brought Willy the soda he asked for, then sat next to him on the sofa. Reggie thought about taking one of the chairs, but that seemed like a dick move and would send the wrong message. He didn't want Willy to think he didn't desire him. The problem was, he was too damned cute for words. "What did you pick?"

Willy pressed start, and Reggie laughed outright. "*A Million Ways to Die in the West*?" A slapstick comedy. "I wouldn't have expected that."

49

"My dad would have a fit if he knew." Willy rubbed his hands together in delight.

Reggie took a swig from his bottle of Corona and sat back. As the movie played, they laughed and groaned at some of the jokes together. About halfway through the movie, Willy leaned against him, and Reggie put his arm around Willy's shoulder. This was so nice, calm, and quiet, gentle… almost domestic.

"I like this," Willy whispered as the credits rolled at the end of the movie. "It's nice just being here with you." He stretched out on the sofa, reminding Reggie of a cat who had just awakened from a nap.

When Willy put his arms over his head, his shirt rode up, treating Reggie to the amazing sight of that strip of glorious pale skin just above his belt. Reggie swallowed to keep from drooling, and Willy shifted to get closer.

"I really do have to go. I have some things I have to do at the church for my dad, and I figure I better break the news to him about my job." The few hours of relaxation for Willy seemed to be over, and as his nervousness returned, it was palpable.

"Look, you can use my guest room again if you want." Reggie knew he was doing the right thing to try to help him. He drew Willy into another hug. "I don't want you feeling this way."

Willy shook his head. "I don't have an excuse this time, and I need to go home and face my father. There is no other way. It's a job, after all. It's not like I'm running away to become a Moonie or something."

"Yeah, I bet your father would have a seizure if you did that."

Willy's chuckle morphed into a full-blown laugh. "That vein in his neck would throb and then his head would explode." He rubbed his hands together. "How fast do you think I can find them?" He was kidding, of course, but it added a few moments of levity. Willy got up, and Reggie did the same, taking care of the bottles and cans, dumping them into the recycling bin.

"Then you should go. But hopefully I'll see you soon." Reggie would have to make sure of it. He walked Willy to the door and said good night before kissing him goodbye. Okay, what started out as a goodbye kiss quickly turned into Reggie pressing Willy to the back of the door in a full-on make-out session that curled his toes. He only pulled away when he ran out of breath. Reggie fumbled a few times getting the door open and stood on the front porch as Willy got in the old car and backed down the drive, then drove away.

Reggie didn't close the door until the taillights could no longer be seen. Then he leaned against the back of the door, still breathing heavily, but he couldn't help smiling. Willy clearly liked him, but he was playing a fairly dangerous game, regardless of how he looked at it. Well, it wasn't too late yet. He could back away and not see Willy anymore. But Reggie knew that was a stupid notion. His heart was already involved, to a degree, and Reggie wasn't the kind of guy who backed down from a fight or from what he wanted. He didn't announce that he was gay, but he wasn't going to deny it either. It was just that if things progressed with Willy, they were going to come to a crossroads, and both of them were going to have to make some hard decisions.

Reggie checked his phone, grateful there were no messages or calls. He also called in to the switchboard just to ensure they knew how to get in touch with him if required, and then he turned out the lights, got undressed, and climbed into bed.

He fell to sleep quickly and was just getting into a wonderful dream starring Willy in a very underdressed state when a persistent beeping pulled him out of it. He snatched his phone off the nightstand and groaned before answering the call as he got dressed once again.

CHAPTER 5

WILLY WENT to work Monday morning. He was nervous but excited. Mr. Webster seemed pleased to have him, and when he showed him the books and what needed to be done, Willy took to it right away. What shocked him more than anything was that his father actually met him that morning and had tea with him before Willy went to work. He hadn't been upset about the job and seemed sort of proud, which was almost hard for Willy to deal with, because his father had never seemed very proud of him for anything.

"There's going to be a lot for you to learn," Mr. Webster said gently, then took him through all the procedures.

"This is no problem," Willy said. He went through the last week's register receipts, balancing everything with the bank deposits and making sure everything was as it should be. Then he got to work on the rest of the books.

"Okay, then," Mr. Webster said that afternoon once Willy had everything entered for the day. He pointed out the weeks' worth of entries he hadn't had a chance to make. The computer system the store had was very good and wasn't hard to learn, just time-consuming. It took Willy two more days to get everything up to date. Mr. Webster was happy, and Willy was pleased. He hadn't seen Reggie since Friday, though, and missed him. Not that he had any real right to, but he did.

By the time Willy left work on Wednesday, he was really tired. He had Thursday off because he was going to be working on Saturday with Mr. Webster. Willy was looking forward to going to his room and spending a few quiet hours alone.

He walked into the house, and his father looked up from his chair, with Mayor Fullerton sitting across from him. It was clear something devastating had happened, but Willy didn't ask. His father wouldn't appreciate his curiosity.

"What am I going to do?" Mayor Fullerton asked, almost begged. "I've been able to keep this quiet for now, but it won't stay that way. You know how people like to talk."

"They already are," his father said, and Willy went through the living room to the kitchen. "I'm afraid it's all over the church and will have spread through the entire town by tonight."

"That sheriff. I swear he has it in for me."

His father tsked. "It's not right to blame someone for doing their job, especially when they aren't at fault."

Willy caught a glimpse of his father's accusatory gaze leveled at Mayor Fullerton. Whatever had happened that had the mayor so upset, his father clearly thought it was the mayor's own fault.

"You let those boys of yours run loose with no supervision. Who knows what kind of influences they've allowed into their lives? Clearly you and Shirley didn't stress to Jamie the necessity of staying on God's path."

Willy sat at the kitchen table while his mother quietly put the finishing touches on dinner. "What happened?" he whispered.

She shook her head and blushed. He hardened his gaze, and eventually his mother sat beside him, glancing toward the living room. "Jamie was picked up by the police a few days ago for doing something he shouldn't out at the rest area." She patted his hand. "You don't need to worry about it—your father is handling things."

"Mom," he whispered. "You have to have your own opinion about stuff." He patted her hand in return. "I know you're smart and worth listening to." He hated the way she had receded into the woodwork since his brother's death.

"He was doing sex stuff with other men," she whispered into his ear. "The poor dear. He had to hide like that and couldn't be himself. Your father thinks it's some bad thing. But...." She stood and went back to work as though she thought she'd said too much. It was the closest to an opinion that differed from his father's that he could remember from her.

Willy stood and went behind his mother at the stove, wrapped his arms around her, and whispered that he loved her before leaving the room.

He went through the living room as quickly and quietly as he could, heading up the stairs. He found Ruthie in Ezekiel's room, reading him a story. She lifted her gaze worriedly, pausing a few seconds before continuing the story. Willy gave them both a smile, went to his room, and closed the door. He called Reggie. "Is it a good time?" he asked, speaking quietly. "The mayor is here with my dad, and I—"

Reggie sighed. "I can't talk right now. But I'll meet you at the house this evening." His voice was robotic.

"Are you alone?" Willy asked.

"No. Everything is fine. I'll see you later." Reggie hung up, and Willy wondered for a second about what he'd been told.

His mother called him to dinner, and Willy got the others and brought them downstairs. The mayor had left, and all five of them sat down at the table. His father said grace in the usual way and then began passing the food.

Willy kept his eyes on his plate, glancing at his father to see if he had any pronouncements to make. Instead, his father asked each of them about their day. Willy told him about work and how much he was enjoying it. Ezekiel explained about finding a mouse in the backyard and how he set it free. Ruthie went on and on about everyone she'd seen and spoken with until their father met her gaze sternly, and she immediately grew quiet. From there the meal continued as normal. Willy cleared the dishes and helped his mother with cleanup before excusing himself. He told her he was going to see a friend and hurried out of the house before his father could want him for anything.

Willy went to his old car. He'd gotten it when he'd gone away to school. Maybe if he did well at work, he could get something better eventually. But Gerty was good enough for now—she got him around.

The driver's door squeaked as he pulled it closed, and he was about to drive away when a rap on the passenger window stopped him. He tensed, hoping it wasn't his father, then lowered the window. "Tony," Willy said with a smile. "What are you doing here?" He opened his door, got out, and hurried around to the other side of the car to hug his friend tightly. "I thought you were in LA?"

"I am—well, I was. I thought I'd take a few days and come home to see my folks. And while I was here, I had to see how you were." Tony smiled that winning smile that had gotten him out of trouble all through school.

"What are you doing now?" Willy asked. "Your mom said a while back that you were doing a commercial or something? I looked for it."

"That fell through. It was supposed to be a national spot, but the casting director wanted me to warm her bed. Of course, I wasn't in a hurry to turn down that sort of thing…." Tony leaned closer, as if imparting a secret. "But then I found out the real deal. There was the possibility of a commercial, and she had been trying out leads for the last month. I wasn't going to get in the middle of a shitshow like that." He sighed. "I'm still waiting tables at a really cool restaurant on Melrose, and I'm doing okay, keeping body and soul together. The owner is wonderful, and as long as I give him notice, he lets me work around auditions." The words flowed from Tony. "It's a pretty good life. I'm young, good-looking"—he posed a little—"and people are starting to take notice. I did bit parts on a soap and a few series. So maybe that will lead to something. Just gotta keep going." He had so much energy, it radiated off him like ripples in a pond. "How are you?" Tony hugged him again. "I've missed you."

"I'm doing okay. I have a job at Webster's. Just started this week. I had to drop out of college, and my dad wants me to follow him into the church." It was his turn to share a secret. "But I don't want to. I'm doing the books, and I think if I can get the money and stuff together, I'll go to online school to finish an accounting degree. I know it isn't as glamorous as what you're doing—"

Tony humphed. "It sounds fun and glamorous, but it's a lot of work and rejection. Still, I have to try. I think I'm pretty good, and all it takes is the right person to see me."

"How long are you here in town?" Willy asked, trying not to check his watch. He wanted to spend some time with Tony, definitely, but Reggie was expecting him.

"Through Saturday. I spent a huge amount of time in the car, so I thought I'd stretch my legs before dinner. I need to get home, but let's have dinner or something. How is tomorrow night? We could go out and have a little fun." Tony lowered his voice. "Is your dad still the way he was?"

"Pretty much." Willy wished things were different for his entire family. "I don't have to work tomorrow."

"Then I'll come by and we can have lunch at my house. Mom was asking about you, and she'd love to see you. I'll come by and pick you up at noon or so. Okay?"

"That would be great."

Tony hugged him again, and Willy went back around, got in the car, and started it up.

Tony grimaced. "That sounds awful. Instead of me picking you up, drive the car down when you come to lunch and I can take a look at it for you." He smiled and stepped away from the car, heading toward his parents' house a quarter mile or so away. Willy had made that walk plenty of times when he and Tony had been in school together. They'd been close, very close, until Tony had graduated from high school and gotten out of town as soon as he could. Still, it would be nice to see his friend again.

Willy put the car in gear. Gerty still ran well, even if she was showing her age on the outside. He turned the car around and pointed Gerty out of town.

Trees towered over the road as he went. Willy liked this drive, leaving town behind and heading up into the pines the town was named for. Most were tall and straight, with some brown spots from the years of drought that had affected the area pretty badly. Thankfully a very wet winter had saturated the ground and the trees had been able to drink their fill. Willy rolled down the window, letting the clean pine and earth scent of the forest fill the car.

He pulled into Reggie's well-lighted drive and parked the car around the back side near the garage. He didn't want questions from anyone who passed about why he was there. Willy hurried to the door and knocked, unable to stop the smile forming on his lips when Reggie answered the door in sweatpants and a T-shirt.

"Come on in," Reggie said. "Did you have dinner?"

"Yeah. It was really strained."

"I don't doubt it." Reggie stepped back, running his fingers nervously through his hair. He closed the door and led Willy to the living room. The eight empty beer bottles on the coffee table told Willy just how wrong things were.

Willy stood beside the sofa, then began gathering the empties and dumped them in the recycling. He also took the old pizza boxes and threw them away. "You want to tell me about it?" Willy sat next to Reggie but got up again, opened the refrigerator, and got a couple of Cokes. When he returned, he opened one and slid the other over to Reggie.

"Okay." Reggie set the beer bottle down, and Willy pushed it away from him. Reggie turned to him, gaze hard, and Willy returned it.

"You don't need to be drunk to talk to me." Willy drank beer, but he was always conscious that his brother had been killed by a drunk driver, and alcohol tended to make him nervous sometimes, so he was careful of the amount. Being around people who were drinking… well, the incident in the club had only confirmed his fear.

"You're right." Reggie squeezed his hand and stood. "I'll be right back." He left the room, and Willy heard water running and maybe the sound of Reggie brushing his teeth.

"Did you clean up?" Willy asked when he returned.

"I took an aspirin and drank some water." Reggie sat back down, and Willy leaned closer, sniffing.

"Minty water," he teased, and Reggie grabbed him, tugging Willy over him, tickling him. Willy squealed and squirmed, trying to get away. "That's not fair." Reggie backed off, and Willy settled against him.

"I needed to hear you laugh," Reggie whispered. "It's been a difficult couple of days."

"Were you hurt or in danger?"

Reggie shook his head. "After you left the last time, I went to bed and got a call almost immediately after falling asleep. A report had come in about some activity out at the rest area on the highway. There have been a number of reports of suspicious activities out there, so I dressed and got into my car, driving right out. When I pulled up, there were maybe half a dozen cars in the lot. A few people left or got into their cars as I passed through. The report called for some activity in the woods. I walked around and shone my light into the trees but saw nothing. By the time I returned, the number of cars in the lot had thinned to three, and I passed a group of women coming out of the ladies' room. I heard them get into their car as I reached the men's room door. I went inside to have a look around."

"Oh God," Willy said softly. "I know what goes on there. I never did anything, but I heard rumors in high school." He put his hand over his mouth. "No…," he whispered.

"Yeah. Jamie Fullerton. He came busting out of the stall, doing up his pants, and nearly ran into me. The man who followed out of the same stall was a little more buttoned up, but it was plain enough what the two of them had been doing. Jamie shook and said nothing, trying to get himself together." Reggie reached for his soda and drank most of it, then burped when he was done. "My intention was to not cause him any more trouble and just have him come out to my car so I could talk to him. I knew how easily this would get around town, and I was hoping to help him. Technically what they were doing was illegal, but very quickly I think I understood Jamie, at least to a degree."

"What happened?"

"Shawn came in. I didn't call him for backup, but he burst inside, took one look, and sneered. He took the other man into custody, so there was no way in hell I could let Jamie go. I loaded him in the car and took him to the station once again." Reggie blew out his breath. "I called the mayor and asked him to come down. The poor man seemed at his wits' end. In the end, we didn't charge either man. The other one was from Nevada, and we let him go with a warning. I gave the same to Jamie, but the damage was done. Shawn gossips like a hen."

"Shoot." Willy leaned against Reggie. "The town is going to go to pieces. I'm surprised I hadn't heard the juicy details already."

"You will. I gave Shawn a lecture about police business remaining police business, and that our personal feelings were not to interfere with the job we did. I told him that he was to speak to no one about anything that happened at the station and to keep his nose out of other people's business. I had hoped that I'd gotten through to him. I even threatened him, asking why he was out at the rest area, casting a few aspersions to keep him quiet."

"Poor Jamie." Willy buried his face in Reggie's shirt. "I understand how he feels. I mean, he knows he's gay, and we all heard about the rest area and the last stall by the window. It was all over the high school. So he went out there to see if...." Willy groaned. "Can you imagine being that hurt and torn up to do something like that?"

"Yeah. Not to mention that he was taking his life and health in his hands. I honestly wanted a chance to talk to him and to try to help him. But Shawn shot that all to hell."

"My dad and the mayor were at the house. My mom told me what happened, in her own way. But I think she heard it from listening to what the men were saying."

"How did your dad take it?" Reggie asked.

"What little I heard sounded like my father was going to make things worse. Take something bad, add a pile of guilt, and make everything and everyone more miserable. He said that it was the mayor's fault for not raising his sons right."

"Son of a bitch!" Reggie swore, leaning forward. "This isn't the 1950s, for Christ's sake. We need to be understanding and help Jamie, not vilify him and his entire family. It isn't something his parents did."

"I know. I'm gay. I can say it now. But the thought of telling my parents scares the complete crap out of me. My father would—" Willy shivered. "I don't know what he'd do."

Reggie held him closer. "You don't know what he'll do when you tell him?"

Willy nodded. "I know I have to eventually. This isn't something that I can keep a secret forever. But I can't tell him now. I'm too dependent on him for so many things. And then who knows what he'll tell Ezekiel and Ruthie? I can live with my dad not talking to me, but I don't want to lose my entire family." Willy lifted his gaze, tears running down his cheeks that he made no effort to disguise.

Reggie sighed. "You know I understand. And you're the one who has the most to lose. I'm the sheriff, and like it or not, they can't fire me for being gay. They could make my life miserable and people could turn away from me. My deputies and the people I work with could make it impossible for me to do my job, and then I'd have to leave." As easily as Reggie said the words, the darkness in his eyes told Willy that Reggie was almost as scared as he was.

Willy took that in and groaned. He didn't want Reggie to go through all that any more than he wanted to run out and announce to his father that he was gay.

"But I'm a big boy—I can make my own decisions and I'll live with them. If people push me around, I can push back. But you have a lot more to lose. You know how your father feels and can guess how he'll react."

Willy wasn't so sure all of that was true. Reggie could say what he wanted, but Willy knew fear, and it was definitely present. Reggie could take care of himself, but that didn't mean he wanted to do it, to be alone all the time and to have to start over because of who he was.

Willy closed his eyes. "Does that mean I don't deserve a life or the chance to be happy?" God, that really sucked.

"No. It means you have to know what the price could be. Jamie is going through all kinds of hell right about now, and if it comes out about you, then you'll be in the same boat he is."

Willy didn't move. "Sounds like a rock and a hard place." He was damned if he did, and lonely, always on the outside looking in, if he didn't. "What do you want?"

"Me?" Reggie asked. "I just said…."

Willy knew what he wanted. He'd known since that day at the club when the amazing man holding him had saved him from God knows what. "I know what I want. It hasn't changed." Willy slid his hand over Reggie's chest. "I know you think I'm some ignorant kid who has no idea how the world works. And maybe I am to a degree, but I know my own mind." He paused, lifting his gaze and pressing his lips to Reggie's, pouring everything he had into that kiss. Willy didn't want to have to tell Reggie what he wanted. He intended to show him.

Without breaking their kiss, Willy shifted to straddle Reggie's legs and hips. Reggie wound his arms around him, cupping his butt in his big, strong hands, sending Willy into throes of ecstasy. No one had touched him like that before, and damn, it was hotter than he ever imagined.

"Willy," Reggie whispered against his lips and ran his hands up his back. "You need to stop a minute."

"Why?" Willy asked with a smile. "I can tell you're into it." That much was obvious.

"That isn't it. Of course I like what's happening. You're a hot young man, and I would have to be a fool or dead not to be turned on by you. But there's more to it than that." Reggie swallowed and cupped Willy's face in his warm hands. "Is this just sex for you? I know that's what you wanted when we first met."

Willy gasped and lightly smacked Reggie on the shoulder. "No. I mean, you're super hot and sexy." He leaned closer. "Is that all you want? I can be okay with that. But I don't think that's what I really want from you." Willy shivered. "I mean, if it's only sex, I can dig that, but I think I want more than that. Maybe you think I don't know what I want or that I'm too young to want to be in a relationship or know what love is…." Dammit, he was rambling, like, a million miles an hour, and Reggie looked at him as though he'd just fallen off the turnip truck and hit his head.

"Hey, sweetheart. You don't need to be nervous. I was just asking what you thought this was for you. I haven't had a relationship in a while, and the last one ended pretty sucky. He was a year or two older than you and suddenly he decided that he wasn't ready for a relationship. He skipped off to go screw half the Bay Area, and I ended up with a broken heart." Reggie ran his thumb over Willy's upper lip, sending a thrill of desire through him. Willy was getting so sexed up, he could barely see straight, and Reggie wanted to talk about shit. "I'm not asking you to give me a forever answer, but let me know what you think is going on."

Willy cupped Reggie's whiskered cheeks in his hands. "I think you're the sexiest, nicest guy I've ever met. You're hot and cool, and you think about me and worry what I think and feel. You could have just fucked me half a dozen times, but you keep holding back because you're worried about me." Willy bit his lower lip. "You do care about me, don't you?"

Reggie held him closer. "Of course I do. But getting involved could have repercussions for you... for both of us. If this is just a sex thing.... Do you think it's worth it? Would Jamie think it was worth it?"

Willy kissed Reggie once more. "I don't know what's going to happen. But I know you're worth it." He pulled up Reggie's shirt and rubbed his chest and belly. "God, this is so worth it. I love a guy with a hairy chest." Willy squirmed as his cock hardened even more, his pants too damn tight. He hoped *that* situation wouldn't last too much longer.

Reggie groaned and lay back on the cushions, his eyes drifting closed, and Willy used that time to explore. To say Reggie was a work of art would be an understatement, though it wasn't like Willy had seen all that much art in his life. Okay, so maybe Reggie was closer to a dream come true. When he closed his eyes and imagined his perfect fantasy guy, it hadn't come close to the glory and heat that was Reggie.

Willy gently stroked Reggie's chest and then down his ridged belly before returning to Reggie's large tawny nipples. He had an urge to see what Reggie tasted like and leaned forward to flick his tongue over the hard bud before sucking lightly. Reggie's slightly salty, hot, hint-of-musk flavor burst on his tongue and filled his nose and sent quakes running all through him. He was touching another man, seeing what he tasted like. Willy let his hands wander down to Reggie's belt. Now all he needed was to….

Heavy footsteps echoed on the porch outside. Willy stopped as they sounded again. Reggie stiffened, and Willy sat back and stood, checking his clothes. Reggie did the same, pulling his shirt down as he crossed the room and peered out around the curtains.

"The mayor," Reggie said softly to warn him. Willy wondered if he should try to hide or something, but it was likely that His Honor could have already seen his car even though he'd parked out by the garage. Shit, what should he do? Flutters of panic welled up inside him, but he took a deep breath and tamped them down. The television remote sat on the coffee table, and he grabbed it, turned on the TV, and flipped through the channels as he held his soda.

A knock sounded, and Reggie wiped his brow before opening the front door.

Willy's heart still beat a mile a second as Reggie greeted Mayor Fullerton and stepped back to let him inside. His thoughts ran a million different directions, but he settled on the fact that he and Reggie were allowed to be friends, and if asked, that's what they were. Go for the simple explanation.

"Sheriff Barnett, I wanted to—"

Willy knew the second he was spotted.

"I'm sorry. I shouldn't have bothered you."

"It's all right. Willy and I were just watching TV and talking. Please come in. Is there something I can do for you?" Reggie motioned Mayor Fullerton to a chair.

"I didn't want to interrupt your evening, but…." He looked so nervous, glancing everywhere like people were going to jump out of the woodwork.

"Please sit down and tell me what's on your mind. I know you've been through a lot lately, and if I can help, I will." Reggie glanced at him, and Willy stood to leave the room. Heck, he should just get ready to go.

"No. Please. I don't want to be a bother." Mayor Fullerton turned to the door.

"It's all right," Willy said.

Mayor Fullerton shrugged. "Yeah, I suppose it is. Everything will be all over town in a matter of seconds. I need to face it and…."

"Sit down," Reggie said, and Mayor Fullerton sat on the edge of one of the chairs.

Willy, needing to make himself useful, got him a glass of water.

Reggie sat in the other chair across from him while Willy went back to the kitchen. He looked through the cupboards and thankfully found a package of Oreos. This most likely wasn't a social call, but there was nothing that said Reggie couldn't be nice to someone hurting. He grabbed a plate, placed a few cookies on it, and brought them to the table.

"I wanted to thank you. Jamie said that when you…. found him, you were nice about it and…."

"Mayor…."

"Please, call me Cal."

Reggie reached for the remote and flipped off the television. "Cal… what happened out there was a cry for help and maybe some attention. From everything I know about Jamie, and it isn't a lot, but all the racing and acting out—it's likely because he's not happy. I see it all the time." He leaned forward, and Willy pulled out one of the stools by the counter and sat down, staying out of the way. "You need to be there for Jamie and listen to what he has to say. Try to see things from his angle."

"How can I? He's…. It goes against God." Cal's voice sounded so hollow, it was frightening.

Willy wanted to jump in and rail against the crap his father spewed all the time. But he held his tongue, too afraid to voice his own opinion, lest it give himself and Reggie away.

"Cal," Reggie said to draw attention back to himself. "Think back. Remember when you first saw Jamie in the hospital after he was born? He was perfect, wasn't he? Beautiful even, and you loved him instantly."

Cal nodded.

"You still love him that same way, don't you? He's still your baby, your little boy."

"Of course he is." Cal's voice showed a little gumption.

"Then that's all there is to it. You love him and you'll do your best for him. It shouldn't matter if he's gay or has brown eyes or three ears. Your job is to love him... period. And remember him like that, because somewhere in the misbehaving, acting-out young man you've been dealing with is that little boy from when you first brought him home."

Cal turned, looking right at Willy. "Your dad doesn't agree with that."

Willy tried to think of what to say.

"The reverend has his opinion. But it's not the only one," Reggie interjected. "I don't share it, and I'll say that straight out. If Jamie is gay, then it's part of who he is. I don't believe it's anything that you or his mother did." Reggie sat back. "I'm sorry I got up on my soapbox, but I think Jamie needs your support and understanding right now."

Cal sighed. "I'm at a complete loss right now, and my wife, she just sits in the kitchen and cries." He stood. "I only came by to thank you for trying to help Jamie. He said you were understanding and...." His voice faltered.

"Please go home and take the time you need with your family. Comfort your wife. Jamie being gay isn't the end of the world, or his world."

"How do you know all this?" Cal stopped at the door, his gaze almost accusatory.

"Because I've spent a lot of time in the outside world. I've seen a lot of kids who need the help and support that Jamie needs. I really hope you'll give it to him." Reggie stood and walked to the door, opened it, and let Mayor Fullerton out. "I have to say that I'm surprised you actually came here. It wasn't something I would have expected."

Cal paused and seemed to teeter for a few seconds. "Sometimes this town can be... insular. A lot of us spend most of our lives here.

We're born and raised here. Young people often leave for better opportunities, but…." He groaned and ran his fingers through his short, slightly graying hair. "I think I wanted an opinion and a perspective from someone different."

"It's understandable, and I hope I was able to help." Reggie extended his hand, and Cal shook it. "Please try to be understanding and gentle with him. And I have to tell you this: you didn't turn your son gay no matter what anyone else thinks."

"But—"

Reggie gently clapped Cal on his shoulder. "You remember that little baby. He was perfect. Well, I'm sure the reverend will tell you that God doesn't make mistakes. So let your son be who he is. And whatever you decide to do, make sure it's your decision, not someone else's."

Cal nodded, and some of the lines from around his eyes smoothed away. "Thank you." He left, and Reggie closed the door, then leaned back on it.

"You were amazing," Willy said as he slipped off the stool. "You helped him, I think. A lot more than my father did."

"I hope so." Reggie stayed where he was.

Willy approached him. "I should go. As much as I want to stay…."

Reggie nodded, his eyes sad. "I know." He turned to look out the front door window. "He knows you were here, and at some point, he'll tell your father. If you stay here too late, your dad will question it." Reggie walked over and engulfed him in a hug. "I'm going to miss you."

"I will come back," Willy said softly. He raised his face and kissed Reggie. "It seems that things are conspiring against us."

"They sure seem to be. If I believed in such things, I'd think the fates were trying to tell us something." Reggie hugged him tighter. "Either that, or you and I are complete fools holding on to something we should probably let go of."

Willy pulled back. "Is that what you want? I know that we can't go walking in town together or be seen going out together, and that sucks. I want to spend time with you, but maybe you're right. Maybe

I'm trying too hard to force something that…." He rested his head on Reggie's chest until Reggie touched his chin. Willy looked up, and Reggie leaned down to kiss him hard, taking possession of him.

Willy quivered from head to foot, unable to think, clinging to Reggie because his entire body came alive just from the kiss. Reggie held him even tighter, his strong arms pressing him to his solid body, heat wrapping around him, encasing him in a cocoon of warmth and safety. Willy knew the safety was an illusion, but he didn't care. In Reggie's arms, it was like nothing could touch him, and he wanted that more than anything.

Reggie pulled back, gazing into his eyes. Willy felt the gaze like a caress, fingers touching his heart.

"I have Sunday off…," he whispered. "My father has to go to a ministerial meeting Sunday afternoon in Tahoe. They do it a few times a year. So I'll try to come see you if I can."

"I'm off too," Reggie whispered, still holding him, not moving.

"Then I'll tell my mom that I'm having lunch with a friend. Dad is usually so busy directly after church…." A thrill of excitement washed over him. "If I can't come, I'll call you." Willy stilled, not wanting to move and leave Reggie's arms.

"I don't want you to get hurt," Reggie told him. "I want to see you, but you have a lot to lose. Please think on what you want, and if you can't come on Sunday or change your mind about—" Reggie's voice broke and he swallowed hard. "I promise I'll understand." Reggie's hug grew gentler, and then he stepped away from him. "Sweetheart, this is your life, and I don't want to make it harder than it has to be."

Willy stifled a groan. His initial reaction was to tell Reggie that he was perfectly capable of making his own decisions, and then the bigger meaning dawned on him. Reggie cared enough to be concerned for him. "I understand that. But I want my life to be full. I don't want to cheat myself and the people I care about just because of what other people might think."

Reggie opened the door, and Willy kissed him quickly before heading back to his life, one that didn't quite seem to fit him most of the time. He turned and waved before reaching his car to go home.

"WHERE WERE you?" his father asked from his living room chair as soon as Willy walked in the door.

"I was with a friend. We watched some television and stuff. Nothing subversive." He rolled his eyes. "If you must know I was at Reggie's, the sheriff. He's a really nice guy." Willy purposely didn't make a big deal out of it. After all, the mayor had been there part of the time, but Willy kept that to himself. What was discussed was no one else's business. "I'm going upstairs." He went through and hugged his mother good night, then climbed the stairs to his room and flopped onto the bed, staring at the ceiling, thinking of Reggie.

The bed bounced, and he caught Ezekiel as he launched his little body upward. "Will you read me a story?" Ezekiel was in his animal pajamas and lay down on the bed next to him.

"How about we find a book and you can read it to me?" Willy offered.

"Okay!" Ezekiel hurried away and returned with a book of Bible stories. He climbed back on the bed and lay next to Willy, opening it to the story of Noah's Ark. He read slowly and carefully, with Willy helping him with a few of the words.

"You're doing great," Willy encouraged, and Ezekiel continued through to the end, smiling.

"Now you read," he said, handing Willy the book, and he found the story of Elijah and read that for him.

"Okay. Go say your good-nights, and I'll tuck you in if you want."

"Mommy will." Ezekiel jumped off the bed, ran to put his book away, and then raced down the stairs.

Willy stood as well, going to the top of the stairs. He heard his dad telling Ezekiel good night. Then their mother brought him up the stairs and took Ezekiel to his room. Willy let the two of them do their thing. It wasn't going to be long before Ezekiel got too old to be read to. Willy was going to miss it.

"How are you?" his mother asked a little while later. Willy had been staring up at the ceiling, thinking of all the things that were going to change.

"I'm fine, Mom."

She sat on the edge of his bed. "I know you're too old to be mothered, but I still worry about you. You dad said you've been spending time with the sheriff." She patted his hand.

"He's a nice guy and he's new in town." Willy scooted back so he could sit up. "What's wrong with that?"

"Nothing, honey." She squeezed his hand. "You need to have more friends, and with the sheriff, I don't have to worry about you getting into trouble." She snickered. "How did you meet him?"

"With Dad. I was at the police station with him and at the courthouse when he went in with Cory and Jamie." He sighed. This whole situation was so difficult. "I wish I knew what I could do to help them. What do you think, Mom?" He looked into her eyes, hoping for something, he wasn't even sure what.

"I think you wanting to help is good. I don't know how you can, though."

"I don't either." Willy sighed again, and his mother leaned forward to kiss him on the forehead.

"I'll see you in the morning." She stood and went to the door. "Don't stay up too late." She left the room, closing the door behind her.

Willy picked up the book on the nightstand, but he kept reading the same page over and over without remembering anything. His phone dinged, and he set the book aside to pick it up off the nightstand. He unlocked it and checked the message. It was from Reggie.

I'm sorry you had to go.

Me too, Willy sent. *But I'll see you on Sunday*, he added with a smile. Then he erased the messages and set the phone on the table once again.

Reggie sent him a smiley face. Willy liked that he had someone to text and talk with. It was like the sun coming out after a rainstorm.

His phone dinged again and he snatched it up. Not many people ever sent him messages.

Is everything okay at home?

Yes. I told my father I was at your house. Who knows how he actually took it? My mom didn't think anything of it. I'm getting tired of worrying about how he feels about everything all the time.

Maybe talk to him? Reggie sent.

Willy sighed. He and his father didn't talk. Well, his father talked, and he was expected to listen.

I'll think about it. Talking to him is like communicating with a brick wall sometimes. He only wants to hear that he's right or have his own thoughts sent back to him. Anyone whose opinion differs from his is wrong. Willy sent the message, then added another. *He wasn't always like that, and I wish he'd go back to what I remember. He used to smile and laugh.*

I wish that for you too, sweetheart, Reggie sent.

Willy smiled. He liked it when Reggie called him that, and he wondered what sort of nickname he could come up with for him.

Willy told Reggie good night and waited for the return message before deleting everything and closing his phone. Then he got up to get ready for bed.

CHAPTER 6

REGGIE WAS more than ready for a day off.

A nurse had come in Thursday to take samples from everyone for drug screenings. The grumblings had been vocal, but Reggie paid no attention to it. He simply explained that this was something police departments did all over the state and that he was just implementing best practices, something that should have been done all along. In the end, he told them to get used to it because it was happening. There were a few glares and final grumbles. What surprised Reggie was that his deputies, none of them, were among the grumblers. It was the support staff.

On Saturday, Reggie had had enough of being in the office. His paperwork was caught up, so he climbed in a car and decided to get his butt moving. He drove through town and then out toward the highway rest area. As he drove out, he passed Shawn coming from the direction of the rest area.

"Marie," Reggie asked once his call connected. "Have there been any reports from the highway rest area?"

"No. It's been quiet out there since you caught Jamie Fullerton. The town is still buzzing about it. Poor dear. I mean, I know that's rather tawdry, but having your bedroom business fodder for gossip is pretty awful."

"I agree. Make sure no one is spreading that sort of thing in the station. It's not professional."

"Well...," she hedged. "Shawn...."

"Yes, I've heard it, and I talked to him already." He shouldn't have had to, but for the second time, Reggie had explained how to treat police business, then put a note in Shawn's file. "Where was Shawn to patrol?"

"The south side of town," Marie answered.

"Thank you." Reggie ended the call and continued out to the rest area. He pulled in as a single car drove out of the lot. Another came in, one very familiar. Reggie opened his door to get out. "What are you doing here?"

"I passed you and saw you coming out here and thought I could say hi." Willy smiled as he closed his car door. Reggie scratched the back of his neck. "Is there something going on out here?"

"I don't know." Reggie sighed. He really wanted Willy to get out of there for his own safety. "I want to take a look around."

"I'll come with you," Willy offered.

Reggie wasn't sure that was a good idea, but it seemed no one else was there, and it would be nice to have some company. It could be that he was being extra suspicious, but that nagging feeling about Shawn never seemed to go away completely.

He walked along the sidewalks and paths, checked out the restroom building and then wandered around back.

"Condoms and stuff," Willy pointed out.

Reggie nodded. He expected that with the place's reputation. He shook his head, keeping an eye out.

"Do you know what you're looking for?" Willy asked, staying close behind him.

"Something that doesn't belong...," Reggie answered. The ground near the building had been well compacted, with trees growing relatively close. After dark, this area would be out of sight to anyone passing, and cars in the lot would seem like they belonged there to use the facilities.

"If someone was going to do something bad, why would they do it here?" Willy pointed. "Why not back in the woods or something? There's lots of space there."

Reggie shrugged. "Because it's most likely that it's a transaction of some sort. I've thought it could be drug deals, but this is a terrible place for that sort of thing. It's out of the way, and the road is only a two-lane highway. It isn't as though Sierra Pines is at a real crossroads. It's still possible...." His voice trailed off as he spotted indentations in the ground, like the start of a trail, leading off into the trees. "Stay here," he said and slowly made his way along the light trail, but it went about forty or fifty yards and stopped. Probably just another route to get farther into the trees for sex. Condom wrappers and waste littered the ground, and he groaned. Reggie should have known this was a dead end, but he'd been curious and wanted to check the place out.

"Anything?" Willy asked.

"No. Go on back to your car. I'll be out there in a minute." Reggie finished looking over the area and found nothing other than ground strewn with pinecones in various states of decay, pine needles, and enough sex debris to have started and kept a whorehouse in good stead for months. Reggie returned to the front of the building. Willy had turned away from him, and Reggie couldn't help admiring his tight little butt encased in nearly new jeans. "Don't you need to work?"

Willy didn't turn around. "I went in early and opened up the store so Mr. Webster could spend some time with his daughter, son, and grandson. I got to leave early, and I saw you coming out here."

"What are you looking at?" Reggie followed his line of sight. There was nothing to see but a few cars passing in the direction of Sierra Pines.

"I don't know."

"What is it?" Reggie pressed.

"I stepped out from the side of the building, and this old van pulled in. It was the kind with the windows all around, except they were covered over on the inside. I probably wouldn't have even noticed except they pulled in, slowed like they were going to park, and then took off fast in the direction they'd come from."

"They could have been turning around," Reggie said with a shrug.

"Except they spun their wheels as soon as they came into view of your car and hightailed it. I could see the driver through the window, and he couldn't get out of here fast enough. It was white with rust, but I didn't get a plate or anything. I didn't know I was seeing anything special until it was over." Willy turned around. "Maybe it was nothing, but it seemed out of the ordinary."

Reggie couldn't argue with that and thought about taking off in pursuit, but he didn't have anything to go on. He couldn't stop them just for turning around. He needed something more concrete, and with the county line less than five miles up the road, they would be out of his jurisdiction before he could catch up with them.

"Is that a camera?" Willy asked, pointing toward the corner of the building, up near the roofline.

"Yes. If it's working." Reggie pulled out his notebook and made a note to see if he could get the footage from the camera from the transportation department. That should be easy enough. Some of that was online now. Not open to the public, but it could be accessed through a secure website. "We can go." He doubted they were going to see anything else today.

Willy turned to him. "I told my dad that I was going to spend some time with friends from Davis and that I was going to go down there tonight. I have a bag packed in my trunk and…. Sorry, it was a dumb idea."

"No. I'm off tomorrow, but I have a few hours yet on my shift, and I want to make sure everyone is aware of what I need them to do while I'm off." Reggie reached into his pocket, pulled out his keys, and handed Willy the one to the house. "If you want some time away, go on to the house. That should unlock the garage as well. Pull your car into the second bay. It's empty. They're calling for some more rain, so…." He knew he was deluding himself, saying to get the car out of the weather. Neither of them wanted the car seen, especially overnight.

"I'll see you in a few hours, then." Willy glanced at the camera and went back to his car.

Reggie returned to his and drove to the office, both excited and nervous about the evening ahead.

REGGIE KNEW that he was entitled to a private life and that it wasn't anyone's business who he spent his time with. He told himself that over and over as he tried to concentrate on his work. He hated that

Willy was lying just to be with him. It wasn't fair. Reggie wanted to be able to stand in the open and say that he liked Willy.

Reggie left the station and walked the main street of Sierra Pines, past the diner with its usual cadre of faces having coffee, the drugstore, and the clothing store. He smiled as he stopped to peer into the knitting shop, where a class seemed to be taking place. He waved in return to a few hands raised his way.

A pair of teenagers walked toward him, holding hands, passing him with a nod. He wanted to be able to do that with Willy. Just seeing his car pull up at the rest area had been like clouds parting. The stress of the day lifted because Willy was there. His heart fluttered and his guts released some of the ever-present pressure that existed because of his job and life. Reggie had had a few boyfriends and a few more encounters, but none of them left him wanting them to come back as soon as they left. With Willy, he couldn't get enough.

"Afternoon, Sheriff," a man Reggie didn't know called as he passed. "Gonna rain, I hear."

"That's what I hear. Stay safe." He returned a smile, and they both continued walking.

Reggie found himself in front of the drugstore and stopped, doing a mental check of what supplies he had at the house. Not that he intended to buy certain kinds of things in town, and definitely not while he was in uniform, but it made him think of it. He went inside, smiling at the woman at the register before heading back through. He ended up in the candy aisle because... well, it was candy, and sometimes he was a kid at heart. Reggie picked up a bag of gummy bears and wandered through the store, getting a few other things.

"Jamie hasn't been out of the house in days from what I hear. Too ashamed to show his face," a female voice floated over the counter. "It's just awful. I know I won't vote for his father in the next election. Personally I think he should resign. Think of the image that sets for our children."

Reggie rolled his eyes, grabbing the can of shaving foam he needed.

"I know. My son told me that all the kids in school are talking about it, and he's in third grade," a second woman said.

"It makes me sick," a deeper voice echoed from the other aisle.

"Well, it would. You're a guy," the first woman said.

Reggie took his purchases around to where a couple of people in jeans and T-shirts stood in the aisle. One wore house slippers and the other flip-flops. "Afternoon," Reggie greeted as he approached, treating the group to pointed stares. He smiled, and they stopped talking, all three of them having the grace to blush. One woman excused herself and hurried away, while the other two waited for him to pass, then whispered back and forth between them.

Reggie approached the counter to find a man in his early forties behind the register. "Sheriff."

"You must be Mr. Webster," Reggie said amicably. He extended his hand and they shook. "I've met an employee of yours, Willy. It's good to meet you." He set his purchases on the counter. "Any troubles?"

Mr. Webster shook his head. "Only the gossips who can't seem to keep their nose out of anyone's business." He spoke louder than was necessary, and Reggie liked him already. "People need to let others live their lives without all that chatter."

"I agree. People have a hard enough time without that kind of judgment." Reggie pulled out his wallet while Mr. Webster rang up his purchases. He handed him a twenty and got his change. "Thank you."

"No. Thank you." Mr. Webster bagged his things and handed them over. "Please stop in again any time."

"I will." Reggie smiled and nodded, leaving the store. The sky had darkened, and clouds hung around the mountains in the distance, trapped there until they dropped their burden and could get light enough to pass over. He hurried back the way he'd come and reached the station as the rain began falling steadily.

"I thought you'd gone," Marie said.

"Just walked through town." Reggie smiled quickly. "I want people to see me and maybe get to know me." He stood next to her at the switchboard. "It means they'll be more likely to call us if they see something suspicious, and it builds a good relationship with the community."

"We already have one," Shawn said with a scowl as he passed.

Reggie was really starting to personally dislike the smug man. "You'd never know it from the look of it," he retorted. "You don't understand. This is a small town—"

"I know what it is. I was born here." Shawn scowled, and Reggie pointed to his office, glaring at him. Shawn tromped inside, and Reggie closed the door.

"I know you think you should have had my job," Reggie said, whirling on him. "But you aren't qualified." He crossed his arms over his chest with a half smile. "You're more interested in your position and how you look than the job you do. The people of this town and the county need to trust us, but they don't trust you." Reggie lowered his arms. "You have the makings of a good law enforcement officer, but you're petty and self-important."

"And you know all that from being here... what, two weeks?" Shawn sneered. "You put out a few bulletins and think you've made a difference?"

Reggie leaned forward. "Actually, that information was in the report I was given by the state justice department when I agreed to take the job. They weren't going to allow you to be sheriff. They were trying to clean up the problems here, not add to them." Reggie kept his voice level. "The thing is, you've done nothing but confirm that their report is correct." He hardened his gaze. "I wonder, can you feel the ice under your feet getting thinner and thinner?" Reggie tilted his head toward the door, and Shawn reached to open it. Reggie waited until he had the door open. "I suggest you consider the type of deputy you want to be and if you want to keep your job or not." Reggie met a gaze that seared with pure hatred. He waited for Shawn to turn away and then sat down to finish up for the day.

REGGIE PULLED up to his house later than he wanted. The lights were on, and instead of the usual cold darkness, it looked and felt warm, like a home. Reggie parked his car outside the bay where he'd asked Willy to park and went inside, dodging raindrops.

His stomach rumbled and he groaned as his senses went into overdrive. "What are you making?" Reggie asked. The scent was incredible.

"Nothing much. I have steaks to put on the grill, and I made some Caesar salad." Willy grinned and pressed a cookbook across the counter. "I made my own dressing. I also have rolls in the oven and glazed carrots."

Reggie hurried over to where Willy stood with a large towel around his waist as an apron. Reggie hugged him, lifting him off his feet, twirling him around. "You're going to spoil me."

"Isn't that what I'm supposed to do?" Willy giggled, and Reggie set him back down, kissing Willy deeply, the taste of the dressing still on his lips from when he'd sampled it. Willy smoothed Reggie's hair back, cradling his head as he kissed him, his tongue exploring Reggie's mouth. Reggie loved that feel and taste.

"You're temptation personified," Reggie whispered.

"Me?" Willy asked, chuckling. "I'm temptation? You're the one with all the muscles and hotness. I'm just a skinny kid from Sierra Pines."

"You're a lot more than that." Reggie held Willy tightly, amazed at how they fit and how quickly he came to treasure their stolen moments together. He had no illusions that this time, their time, was stolen… and he didn't know how much longer they were going to be able to continue.

"Tell me," Willy whispered.

"Sweetheart, you're adorably cute, and you have the biggest heart of anyone I have ever met." They could have ordered pizza or heated up something, but Willy was making a dinner fit for a king, and Reggie felt like one. "The last person to cook for me before you was my mom."

"I'm not surprised. Most of the pans and stuff are still new." Willy slipped away, and Reggie missed his touch immediately. The wind and rain buffeted the windows, and Reggie peered outside as

Willy went back to work. "Go get cleaned up, and then maybe you can build a fire. It's supposed to get cold and damp tonight. I'll have dinner for you when you come back out."

Reggie didn't want to leave the room. One minute away from Willy was a minute too much. He stole another kiss from those sweet, full lips and then hurried down to his bedroom.

He took care of his uniform and gun before going into the bathroom and starting the shower. He stepped under the spray and soaped himself up, hands wandering over his skin. Within seconds he was hard and throbbing, and all it had taken was the single thought of Willy in here with him, Reggie's hands gliding over that smooth, lithe body. He groaned and gripped his cock hard, sliding his soapy hands over it. "Shit," he whispered. As much as he wanted to come, he had Willy out in the other room, and he was spending the night. Now, that didn't mean that anything was necessarily going to happen, but it was pretty clear that Willy cared for him, and….

Reggie needed to think about someone other than Willy so he could finish his shower without coming all over the tile. He twisted the tap to cold to decrease the temperature and rinsed off the soap, shivering. Still, he got his body under control and turned off the water. Stepping out, he grabbed a towel to get warm and dried off quickly to get the cool water off his skin.

In the bedroom, he pulled on comfortable clothes and slid his feet into slippers before joining Willy in the main room, where a fire crackled in the fireplace. "I thought you wanted me to do that?"

Willy grinned. "I had a few minutes and found the wood outside the back door." Willy motioned for Reggie to have a seat and brought the salad bowls to the coffee table, then returned for two glasses of iced water. "I couldn't find any wine and I didn't want to have beer."

"This is good." Reggie sat down with Willy right next to him, half leaning against him as they ate. "Man, it's tangy." He grinned.

"The anchovy. You don't have to put a lot in because you don't want the dressing to taste fishy, but it gives it that tingle that dances on your tongue." Willy took a bite, swallowed, and then leaned in to kiss him. "See, tingle."

Reggie bumped his shoulder. "Maybe we should try that again." He took a bite and repeated the process, kissing Willy. Damned if his lips didn't vibrate just a little. Reggie attributed it to the man he was kissing rather than salad dressing.

They finished their dishes, and Reggie took care of the bowls while Willy served the next course. "Where did you get all this?"

Willy rolled his eyes. "At the store. Where else?"

"I understand that, but it must have cost a lot, and I don't want you using your hard-earned money to feed me." Reggie knew this was tricky, but Willy had just started his job, and the food easily could've cost him a good part of a day's pay, judging by the steaks he put on the plate.

"I didn't do this to be paid back. But…."

Reggie put his arm around him when he sat back down. "I know. I just don't want to cause you hardship or make you sad. So I'll make you a deal—you cooked, so I'll pay." He nuzzled Willy's neck. "Please." The last thing he wanted was for Willy to feel bad.

"Nobody ever thinks about how I feel." Willy brought over the plates, and they sat once again after Willy put another log on the fire.

"I'm sorry," Reggie said.

"I had friends in school who listened to me. They were pretty cool. When I had to withdraw, I lost a lot of that kind of support and contact. I had my own life there, and when I came back here, my family expected me to be the same as when I left, but I wasn't. My dad seemed to want to make all my decisions for me, just like when I was a child." Willy blinked. "But he seems happier for me now."

"Maybe it was because you weren't independent enough?" Reggie offered. "I mean, your father is a very different kind of man. I don't think I've met many like him… ever."

"Let's hope not," Willy snarked, and Reggie smiled.

"Let me ask you something. What does your father want?" Reggie ate slowly, letting the savory flavor of the meat linger on his tongue, then following it with the sweet of the carrots. It was a sublime combination, and he hummed under his breath, closing his eyes. Perfection.

Willy ate as well. "I know he thinks he loves me and wants the best for me. Or what he thinks is the best for me. I have to question how he goes about it."

Reggie couldn't argue with that.

"But he's been supportive, and I don't want to say proud of me, but encouraging since I got the job. He still acts like he did." Willy set down his fork. "At least he's predictable to a large degree." Willy forked up another bite. "What's your dad like?"

Reggie chuckled. "My dad was all about working hard and looking for opportunities. At first he wasn't particularly thrilled when I wanted to be a police officer. He'd hoped I'd be a lawyer or a doctor. That was his dream. The two of us discussed things, and in the end, he agreed that it was my life. I think he still worries about me a lot. I know my mom does, but they're proud of me too."

"Did you see them when you were in the city?" Willy smiled as he chewed a bite of carrots.

"Oh yeah. We went out to dinner and spent some time together. Mom and Dad now have a really busy social schedule. Dad spent so many years as a mail carrier during the day, and he spent his evenings forging knives and things like that. He loved it and still does. Some of his knives go for thousands of dollars. He's a real down-to-earth man, but we never doubted for a second that he loved us. He was busy, but he was always there to put us in bed when we were kids." Reggie hummed softly as he thought back. "I'd love for you to meet them." And just like that, he was thinking further out, hoping for more with Willy. That was dangerous, but his heart beat a little faster at the thought.

"What about your mom?" Willy smiled. "You got this look when you mentioned her."

Reggie chuckled. "My mom is a hoot. She's one of those mothers who believed that time was precious. Dad had to work a lot and couldn't always get weekends off and stuff. But Mom was fierce. She took us camping in Yosemite more than once. She loved that place with the rock domes. I swear she would have been a climber if she could have. Yosemite Falls was a favorite spot too. We'd visit

81

and hike all around. She took us to see the sequoia, and then when we came up here, she would organize day hikes on trails and through the woods. Nothing ever seemed to stop her. She wanted Janine and me to love the outdoors and to see as much of the world as possible." Reggie adored his mother. "She's, like, my hero."

"It sounds like it," Willy said softly. "My mom has grown so quiet. It's like she's a different person since my brother died."

"Maybe she is. That kind of grief doesn't just go away. It lingers and changes people. You said it changed your dad."

Willy nodded. "Please... I didn't mean to interrupt." He cut a bite of steak and chewed while Reggie got his thoughts together.

"Here's a good one. My mom went to work when I was fourteen. She got tired of sitting at home and wanted to get out. She took a job in the office of a manufacturer. They made small, detailed parts for airplanes. She answered phones, filed, and basically managed the office because her boss was terribly unorganized, and she kept him productive. Anyway, Mom saved the money she made. She and Dad lived off what Dad made, and she banked what she had. So, when Janine got the chance to go to France with the foreign language club, Mom sent her. And when I got the chance to go to Europe with the band, she paid for that. Mom also helped us with college and made sure both of us got a good education." Reggie wiped his eyes. "I owe a lot to my mom." He finished his dinner and set down his fork, leaning back. He closed his eyes and waited while Willy finished eating before clearing the dishes and taking them to the kitchen.

Reggie cleaned up, loading the dishwasher and letting Willy relax, consciously aware of him the entire time. It was like he had some sort of Willy radar. Even when he stood to go to the window, Reggie knew where he was. "You can watch television if you like," Reggie offered, not wanting Willy to be bored.

Willy wandered through the house to the back, the door snicking closed after him. Reggie finished the last of the cleanup and slipped out as well, stepping out onto the covered deck. Willy stood at the edge, leaning on the log rail, staring out over the backyard and forest that rose like a wall with the Sierras looming above.

"What are you thinking about?" Reggie asked, sliding his arms around Willy's waist.

Willy shrugged. "I keep wondering what you can see in me, and then I see you look at me and...." He quivered, and Reggie held him tighter. "When you first approached me in the club in Sacramento, I thought maybe you were like those guys who were ganging up on me, but you weren't. You were kind and you tried to help me." Willy leaned back against him. "When you left, I was lonely. I actually kicked myself for the rest of the night because I let you get away."

"I'm right here."

"I know, and I'm scared." That was quite an admission. "I'm scared of what will happen if people find out about us, and I'm scared that I'm going to have to spend the rest of my life hiding who I am. I know I can't do both."

"You don't have to make that decision today." Reggie leaned forward to gently kiss the base of Willy's neck. Willy shivered, and Reggie did it again.

"Reggie... I...." Willy groaned as Reggie tugged his shirt aside, kissing down his shoulder.

"I know this is your first time and I want to make it special for you." A breeze off the mountains chilled its way around them, and Reggie gently led Willy back inside. He closed the door, and they returned to the living room. While Willy got comfortable on the sofa, Reggie built the fire back up and then sat next to him. "We don't have to do anything you aren't comfortable with." Reggie took Willy's hands, threading his fingers through them, soft skin sliding along Reggie's rough fingers. "I mean it. We don't have to do anything if you aren't ready." Reggie tugged him closer, their lips close but not touching. "I'd be happy just being able to hold you tonight." Their first night together. He didn't need to even think of the other side of that coin.

Willy closed the distance between them, and Reggie wound his arms around him. He hadn't gotten an answer, and that was fine. Willy didn't need to vocalize what he wanted right now. Reggie had every intention of taking his time, making sure Willy had a first time to remember for the rest of his life. "I don't even know what to do," Willy whispered. "I know it sounds dumb of me, but all I've ever done is hear guys talking about it, and I doubt they knew very much about what they were doing."

"You're probably right. They didn't."

"And they were all talking about girls." Willy grinned. "I always felt sorry for the girls they were dating because of the way they talked about them. Like there was nothing private or sacred."

"What happens between us is both." Reggie slid closer, holding Willy tighter, following his gaze to the flickering flames. "I will never talk about what goes on between us with anyone except you."

"It's not that." Willy turned to him. "I'm scared."

"Of what?" Reggie wondered.

"Sex, I guess. Never had it, and everyone talks about it like it's the greatest thing ever, but it's the cause of so much trouble and pain that…." Willy trailed off as Reggie drew closer, their breath mingling and then lips touching. Reggie held him firmly, deepening the kiss until Willy moaned softly and the return kiss grew more urgent. He backed away, tugging on Willy's lower lip as he did.

"Does that scare you?" Reggie asked, and Willy shook his head. Reggie pulled Willy's shirt up, taking a good look at his pale, smooth belly and chest. Just as he'd imagined, only better, more heated. He touched his lips to Willy's upper arm, then downward and captured a nipple, sucking and teasing it with his tongue to the tune of Willy's higher-pitched, more urgent whimpers. "How about that?"

"No. But I think…."

Reggie rested his head on Willy's shoulder, his lips inches from his ear. "We don't have to do that. This is about happiness, feeling good, being together. Not worry and fear. Sex should never be that." He licked the spot right behind Willy's ear, and Willy shook in his arms, groaning softly once again. "Those sounds."

"Am I being too loud?" Willy stiffened.

"No, sweetheart. They're beautiful. Like fine music. You make as much noise as you want." Reggie went back to exploring Willy's body, finding the spot at the base of his neck and the one along his shoulder that made him gasp. Reggie tugged off Willy's shirt, pressing him back onto the sofa cushions. Willy's belly heaved up and down, his small pink nipples peaked in the cold. Reggie stroked him gently, Willy's smooth skin heating his palm. "You're stunning."

Willy shook his head. "I'm plain and ordinary. Just say it like it is."

"There—" Reggie leaned forward, taking his lips, sucking lightly. "—is nothing—" He gently kissed the base of his neck. "—ordinary about you." He gently kissed Willy's shoulder. "You're extraordinary and special." He leaned closer, inhaling deeply just to take in more of the scent of heaven that was Willy. Reggie stayed where he was without moving for a few seconds. He needed Willy to hug him, move, anything.

Reggie sighed as Willy encircled him, pulling them together. It took Reggie a few seconds to get his own shirt off, and then Willy held him once again. Chest to chest, heat to warmth, they pressed together, Reggie finding Willy's lips, their kisses driving him, adding passion by the second. His instinct pushed him forward, to take Willy, but he'd be damned if he was going to do that. Things had to happen at Willy's pace, not his. And when Willy kissed the base of his neck that way Reggie had kissed his just a few seconds before, Reggie backed away and tugged Willy on top of him.

Willy grinned. "Am I in charge? Is that it?" He placed his hands on Reggie's shoulders and slowly slid them down his chest. Willy didn't say anything, his chest rising and falling with each breath, fingers trembling as they moved.

"You aren't going to hurt me." Reggie covered Willy's hands with his own and brought one to his lips. "I mean it. I want you to get to know me, feel comfortable touching and being touched." He squeezed Willy's fingers, then released them and lay back, reveling in the gentle feeling of Willy touching him.

Reggie held his breath as Willy circled his nipple with his finger and tweaked the bud lightly. He arched his back into the sensation, groaning softly under his breath to let Willy know that he liked it. Willy continued his explorations, sliding his hands down Reggie's belly and then over to his side. Reggie chuckled, even as his excitement went through the roof. He closed his eyes, willing Willy to free his erection and touch him. When Willy slid his hand close to his waistband, Reggie held his belly still, pulling it in. Willy teased him, running his fingers along his stomach before stopping.

Willy kissed him, pressing his chest to Reggie's, mingling their heat. "I'm not sure what I'm supposed to do."

Reggie chuckled and slid his hands down Willy's back to cup his butt and massage his cheeks through his pants. "You can touch whatever you want to."

Willy sighed and sat back. "Do you want to do this here on the sofa?"

Reggie shook his head. The fire was burning down, so he stood, settled the wood, and then sat once again. "We should let it burn down a little more." The last thing he wanted was for a spark to get loose while they weren't there.

Reggie tugged Willy to him, and they sat quietly together, fingers intertwined as they watched the flames die. As the room chilled and the fire flickered out, Reggie stood and offered his hand. Willy took it, and Reggie led him out of the living room, turning out all the lights as they went down to the bedroom, and shut the door behind them.

They were in his room, his space. Reggie never let anyone else in here. This was his sanctuary. The rest of the house had touches of his uncle still about, but this room was all him. Reggie guided Willy to the bed and down onto the thick duvet. He kicked off his shoes and took off his socks before sliding down his sweatpants and briefs. Reggie shoved them to the side and stood in front of Willy, naked. He was who he was, stripped bare. Most people thought nothing of this, but for Reggie it meant a lot. He was himself, and Willy could see it.

Willy leaned forward to take his hand, drawing him closer until their lips met in a searing kiss that made the floor shake like no earthquake he'd ever felt.

"I think it's my turn," Willy said, standing. He pushed Reggie away slightly and he took a step back. Willy toed off his shoes and took off his socks. Then he turned around, pushing down his jeans, showing Reggie his butt clad in light blue briefs. It was like waving a red cape in front of a bull. Willy had an amazing posterior, and when that fabric slipped downward and then off, Reggie gasped and held his breath.

Slowly Willy turned around.

"I told you. Amazing," Reggie said, and Willy shook his head. Reggie slowly walked around Willy. He gently pressed to his back, snaking his arms around his waist, holding him, kissing the base of his neck. "You are stunning." He was rock-hard, his cock pressing to Willy's butt. "You can feel me, can't you?"

Willy giggled. "Yeah."

"That's what you do to me." Reggie closed his eyes, inhaling, letting Willy's scent carry him away on clouds of ecstasy for a few split seconds. "You don't have to worry about how you look. I think it's wonderful." He stepped back slightly, kissing Willy's shoulder blade as he rubbed small circles on his belly. "I know it's hard to let someone else see you, the real you."

"What do you mean?"

Reggie held Willy tighter. "We spend our lives hiding parts of ourselves. We learn about it on the playground at school. The kids who are different get picked on. You don't have the right clothes or your nose is too big or you wear glasses. The kids who get picked on usually change some part of themselves, hiding what they really like to become part of the group. As we get older, we do it more. Our bodies look funny or our face gets spots or God knows what else…. We don't think we're smart enough or whatever. We hide more and try to present a better picture of ourselves, the one we want the world to see." Reggie held his hands to Willy's chest, cradling him in his arms. "Standing in front of someone naked, especially someone we want to be intimate with, is shedding part of that image. We let someone else see who we are."

Willy coughed and then cleared his throat. "But what if the other person doesn't like what they see?"

Reggie chuckled. "Then fuck that and kick 'em in the nuts because they aren't worth bothering with." He kissed Willy's shoulder once again. "I like what I see. I knew I would."

"How can you?" Willy glanced down.

"Because what really counts is what's on the inside."

"How do you know all this?" Willy slowly turned himself in Reggie's embrace.

Reggie gently cupped Willy's jaw. "Because part of my job is to get to the person under the façade. You look for clues as to who the real person is. That's what motivates our real desires and what we really want. It's also the part of us that usually commits a crime. So, it's what I look for." He kissed Willy deep, pressing their hips together, cocks sliding along each other.

Willy moaned softly, whimpering. "Reggie...."

"You make me feel good." He pushed Willy back toward the bed, lifted him off his feet and turned so he sat, and then lay back, letting Willy be on top and have the control. Reggie cupped Willy's bare, pert butt, holding him firmly, guiding him as he slid along him, cocks touching, Willy moaning softly in his ear. That was almost enough to send him over the edge right there. Willy's pleasure enraptured him, and he let Willy set the pace as they moved together.

"Reggie... oh...." Willy's words and whimpers barely reached Reggie's ears.

"It's okay, sweetheart. Be happy and let go." He held him closer, rocking with him until Willy gasped, head thrown back, mouth open. Heat spilled between them, and Reggie closed his eyes, tumbling right along with Willy. It was an amazing experience being someone's first, and as Willy settled in his arms, Reggie lay still, letting him catch his breath.

"That was…." Willy lifted his head, a huge grin on his face. "I feel almost wicked."

"Maybe you are." Reggie rolled Willy onto his back, sweeping a hand over his forehead. "I'll be right back. Just get comfortable." Reggie hurried to the bathroom, got a cloth and towel, and used them to gently clean Willy's alabaster skin. After taking the used linens back to the bathroom, he returned to Willy's eyes following his every movement.

"You're the one who's gorgeous," Willy told him as Reggie approached the bed.

"Get under the covers, Rabbit." Reggie smiled as Willy's eyes went wide.

"What did you call me?" He sat up, arms folded over his chest. "Rabbit?"

"Yeah. It's how I thought of you in Sacramento. You were adorably cute and completely out of your depth. From the second you walked into that club, your eyes were wide and you seemed so innocent and gentle compared to all the jaded guys around you. That's why those men approached you. They figured they could intimidate and get you to do what they wanted." Reggie sat next to him. "When I was a kid, my first pet was a rabbit. His name was Rupert and he was the best pet ever. He was gentle, playful, and a joy to have around. Just like you." He took one of Willy's hands.

"I don't know if I like it."

Reggie laughed. "How about you hop in bed before you get cold and we'll talk about it."

"Har-har," Willy said as he climbed under the covers. "The only reason I'm doing this is because I'm getting cold and I don't want my bits to shrivel up." Willy settled under the covers, and Reggie turned out the lights and climbed into bed next to him, sliding his arms around him.

Reggie closed his eyes, listening to Willy breathe, wondering how much sleep either of them was going to get. Reggie was still really keyed up, but it didn't take long before the fatigue of his day overwhelmed the excitement of having Willy in his bed. He drifted off to sleep, still wondering how much longer this interlude, these stolen hours, could possibly last. He wanted them to, but that had little bearing on reality, which often had its own ideas.

CHAPTER 7

THE GOSSIP through town was enough to drive Willy out of his mind. All anyone was talking about was Jamie Fullerton, and it bothered him. Usually talk in town died down once something else happened, but not this time. It had been nearly a week and the chatter continued.

Willy pulled the cart of boxes out of the back room. He wanted to replenish some displays while it was slow. He was careful as he passed Mrs. Weathers and Mrs. Gardner, talking quietly in the aisle. He wasn't intent on listening to their conversation, but he couldn't help hearing.

"I heard that some people are circulating a petition to have the mayor recalled. I don't know if things should go that far, but apparently Jamie is so ashamed of himself," Mrs. Gardner was saying.

"As he should be," Mrs. Weathers interjected.

"Oh, please." Mrs. Gardner rolled her eyes as Willy passed, leaving them behind. "So the kid is gay. It's hardly the end of the world."

Willy smiled. *Good for you, Mrs. G. I always liked you.* He kept going, and a few seconds later, Mrs. Gardner, in a snit, walked past him up to the counter, with Mrs. Weathers following shortly behind with an expression like she'd just smelled something bad. This was getting ridiculous. He wanted to tell them it was none of their business and to leave it alone.

"Morning," Willy called as a customer came in the store. He didn't pay a great deal of attention as he popped open a case of Peanut M&M's. Mr. Webster was having a sale, and it seemed the town needed as much comfort food as it could get, because they were flying off the shelves. "Jamie," Willy said when he glanced up and saw the other man, looking like he wished the floor would open and swallow him up.

"Mom sent me in for some things and—" He turned and hurried toward the back of the store. Willy wished he could help.

The bell on the door chimed again, and Willy tried to stop the smile that rose to his lips as Reggie entered, in his uniform, looking sexy as all get-out. The first thing that went through Willy's mind was that the next time he saw him, maybe he could get Reggie to wear his uniform and…. Willy blinked away the thought. He was at work, and a stiffy wasn't going to be a good idea. He could already feel the heat rising to his cheeks, and he had to look away and get his mind on what he was doing.

Willy began placing bags of candy on the endcap even as his mind flashed into darkness, the middle of the night. He was awake, staring at the ceiling. He'd just rolled over for the dozenth time. Reggie stirred next to him. He expected to be told to lie still, but heated hands slid over his chest and belly, and then Reggie rolled on top of him, cradling him. Reggie had kissed him until his eyes crossed before slipping down, under the covers, and the angels sang in Willy's mind when Reggie engulfed him in the wettest heat Willy could possibly imagine. It was his first blow job, and Willy's blush intensified as he thought he might actually have squealed when Reggie brought him over the edge.

"Willy."

He turned to Mr. Webster, keeping the boxes in front of him; otherwise he was going to put on quite a show, and there was only one person he wanted to see him that way. "Sorry." He blinked.

"When you're done there, could you make a pass through the back of the store? I need to work in the back for a while and make sure everything is running smoothly in the pharmacy." Mr. Webster was smiling. "It looks like it's going to be a good day." The store was getting busier by the second, which was very unusual for a Tuesday morning.

"Sure, no problem." Willy turned to finish up what he was doing and filled the next display before heading to the back with the cart. Then he did as Mr. Webster asked, walking the various aisles, making his presence known in case anyone needed help.

"You should be ashamed!" A voice, male and growly, carried over the counters. Willy hurried over as a second echoed the sentiment.

"You and your kind aren't welcome here. Maybe you should leave. Go to San Francisco with all the other freaks!"

Willy rounded the corner to where Jamie was cornered by Mark Jeffries and Scott Phillips, two of the star football players when he'd been in school and two of the biggest, loudest assholes he'd ever met in his life. Those two were joined at the hip, and their mission had been to make everyone's life as big a hell as possible.

"That's enough, both of you," Reggie said as he stepped up, feet wide, the man a brick wall of not taking crap from anyone. "Don't you have places you need to be?"

Scott, the lead asshole, turned to Reggie with a sneer. "Nope. We're fine right here. He's the one who's a problem." He pointed at Jamie, who stood as tall as he could, trying to hold together some of his dignity.

"I suggest that you two quit causing trouble and move on, now." Reggie was strong, and Willy puffed his chest out in pride for him. He wasn't going to let them get away with their usual crap.

"You're going to stick up for a fag like him?" Scott pressed. "I can't believe it. We got ourselves a fag-loving sheriff."

"That's enough," Mr. Webster said, stepping into the fray from the back of the store. "We'll have none of your mouth in here." He turned to Reggie and then back to the troublemakers. "I don't want to see either of the two of you in the store any longer. And I'll be calling your parents just to make sure they know you aren't welcome and why. Your behavior is disgraceful." He was such a great guy. Willy felt honored to work for him. "If they come back, I want them charged with trespassing."

"You heard him," Reggie said. "I suggest you leave now, or I will arrest you and charge you with trespassing. We'll see if a nice cell will cool the two of you off."

Scott's resolve crumbled as Willy watched. He must have seen his position was hopeless. He'd been called out in a huge way, and the bully wasn't going to be able to stand up to it. Not really. He stormed toward the front door, with Mark following behind him and everyone else sort of tagging along like a wave driven by curiosity, the possibility of a proverbial train wreck pulling them all in the same direction. Scott left the store, the door sliding open and then closing behind him.

Mark turned to Reggie, aiming a look of such venom and hatred that Willy nearly took a step back. "The only people who stand up for faggots are other faggots." He sneered, and Willy stood stock-still, fear planting his feet in place. He took a step back to get out of the line of verbal fire when he saw a twitch in Reggie's cheek. It was barely noticeable, but it was there. If he hadn't been looking so closely at Reggie, Willy probably would never have seen it, but it was the only indication as far as Willy could see of just how dead-on Mark's arrow truly was.

"Leave right now," Reggie said. "That's enough out of that foul mouth of yours. One more word and I'll take you in for threatening a police officer."

Mark stared back at Reggie and then slowly turned, an unreadable little smile on his lips. He took a final step, and the front door slid open. Mark stepped outside, and Reggie followed him. The door slipped closed, blocking out the sounds from the street, leaving the store in an envelope of silence and shock.

Mr. Webster broke it. "Okay. Let's get back to work."

Willy nodded and looked around to get his bearings and try to get his mind to process the next item he needed to work on.

"I'm sorry, Mr. Webster. I should have just stayed home," Jamie said as Reggie came back inside. "I'm sorry," he repeated to Reggie, his head down, cheeks reddening. Willy felt so bad for him. The cocky, misbehaving kid he'd been seemed to have flown out the window. Between the stuff with the racing and now the revelation from the rest area, it was hard to believe he was the same person.

And maybe he wasn't. The conversation from the night before flashed through Willy's mind. Could it be that someone could build the image they wanted the world to see and hide behind it so well that when it was gone, there was nothing left?

"Nothing for you to apologize for," Reggie said, "except the motorcycle racing. The rest of it, well, that's people being small and petty."

Jamie nodded. "Let me get what I came here for and I'll get out of everyone's hair." He walked quickly toward the back of the store.

Willy shook his head and returned to the tasks at hand.

"Is there something I can help you with, Sheriff?" Mr. Webster asked.

"I was stopping in to get some chocolate for my desk at work, and things got a little sidetracked." Reggie wandered off as well.

Willy made sure Rose was okay at the register. She was retired and worked part-time to supplement her income. Then he went to the back room to bring out more product to fill the shelves. His job had become sort of a catchall once he had the books done. Willy wasn't going to complain at all. It meant he got to work more hours and it kept him busy.

In the back, he filled the cart with cases once again and pulled it back to the floor. As he stepped through the swinging door, he nearly collided with Jamie. He excused himself, continued on down the second aisle, and got to work, moving toward the back as he went.

"Sheriff," Jamie said softly from down the next aisle. Willy stilled, knowing he shouldn't be listening in. "Can I ask you something?" He sounded so nervous, but with a hint of hope in his voice.

"Of course," Reggie answered. "For the record, I'm sorry you're going through this. I did my best to try to prevent it."

"I know. Ummm... about that and what Mark said... I saw your face...."

Willy's stomach clenched and he took a deep breath.

"Yes?" Reggie prodded.

"How well do you understand what I'm trying to work through? I don't know anyone else, and...." Jamie gasped. "I'm sorry. I shouldn't have asked anything like that. It was completely stupid and none of my business, and—"

Willy was afraid to move an inch.

"I understand what you're going through very well. I've been through it myself. You have to decide who you want to be and if you want to be a victim or tackle things head-on. Hold your shoulders back and your head high and own who you are." Reggie's words made Willy proud and ashamed at the same time.

"Do you own who you are?" Jamie asked.

"I answered your question."

It grew quiet for a few seconds, and Willy cleared his throat as he opened a box and started filling shelves. He tried not to think too hard about what had just happened, but it was nearly impossible. Reggie had just outed himself to Jamie Fullerton. Willy understood why he'd done it. Reggie hadn't wanted Jamie to feel so alone. He'd wanted him to know that there was someone else in town who understood. Willy was fully aware of how that felt. But if Jamie knew, then it was only a matter of time before other people found out that the sheriff was gay, and tongues would wag all over town.

Willy knew Reggie was right. The best thing to do was to own up to who you were and let the chips fall where they may. If people didn't understand, then fuck them. But Willy didn't have that luxury. If his father learned that he was gay and that he'd been seeing the sheriff, lying about it…. There would be hell to pay, make no mistake.

"Willy," Reggie said as he came around the end of the aisle. "You doing okay?" He smiled, keeping his tone normal, but Willy felt anything but normal. His plans for trying to be independent and build the basics of a life separate from his father before this came out had just gone up in smoke.

"I don't know," he answered, looking squarely at Reggie, his heart breaking a little as the air around him chilled and he realized the companionship that had filled his days with warmth was turning cold. "Are you okay? Maybe a little feverish?" He raised his eyebrows. "Took leave of your senses?" he whispered, and Reggie nodded.

"You heard that?" Reggie whispered, and Willy nodded slowly. "Come to the house for a few minutes after work."

Willy turned away and shook his head. "I can't." He continued filling the shelves, only half watching what he was doing. "I don't dare." He broke down the box and opened another one.

"Willy, why don't you take your break?" Mr. Webster said.

"Okay." Willy took the cart to the back room, leaving it loaded, and went out through the back door to the small parking lot behind the store. He closed the door and leaned against the building. Reggie had said that he cared for him. Hell, the other night he'd made Willy feel like he was the center of the universe. Of course, he should have known that was an illusion. He was just some dumb kid after all.

Willy wrapped his arms around himself to ward off the chill that rose from inside.

Reggie's cruiser pulled into the lot and parked nearby. He got out and strode across to where Willy stood. "I know you're scared, and I don't blame you, but I couldn't let Jamie believe he was all alone. He's so lost—"

"I get it, I do. You felt for him, and that does you credit. But in case you haven't figured it out, I'm the one who's now all alone. At least Jamie has his dad, who seems to be supporting him. My family never will, and I really don't want to be homeless, so I'm sorry if I'm not dancing a jig or running through town waving those rainbow flags." He looked around, thankful the lot was nearly empty and the area deserted except for them.

"I know you're scared—"

"I'm terrified! You've seen my back. You know what my father is capable of. What if he decides to beat the devil out of me or some such demented thing?" Willy hardened his gaze even as Reggie softened his. "No. I'm sorry. But I can't come out to your house after work, or ever. And it isn't going to matter anyway. Things have a way of getting out, and as soon as it does, my dad will move heaven and earth to make sure I never see you again outside of an official capacity." Willy's legs shook. He'd been counting on Reggie's support, and that had evaporated like the fog against the sun. "Just go back to work. I have only a few minutes more, and then I have things I have to do. I can't afford to lose this job. It's the only thing I have that's my own right now."

He tried like hell not to gaze into Reggie's eyes, and failed. They were filled with just as much hurt as had taken up residence in Willy's gut. His heart ached, and there wasn't a damn thing he could do about it now. Reggie had been Reggie—he'd tried to help someone. That was Reggie's nature and part of why Willy had fallen for him so quickly.

Willy turned away, opened the back door, and returned to the stockroom, shutting the door behind him. He locked it and went to the restroom, closing and locking the door before leaning against it, breathing deeply. He had to get himself together enough that he could work through the rest of the day. After he closed up and went home or wherever he could find to think, then he could fall apart.

WILLY WASN'T interested in going home after work. He needed some time to deal with what had happened, and he didn't think that would be possible there. Willy could imagine his father waiting up to talk to him… or talk *at* him was more like it.

He went to his car, turned out of the parking area onto the main street, and just kept going. The streetlights flashed past, growing more distant and then nonexistent as he left the town farther behind.

He was alone, physically as well as emotionally, the town in the distance behind him just like the relationship he'd thought he was building with Reggie.

Lights to the right caught his attention, and Willy realized he was coming up on the rest area he and Reggie had explored that previous Saturday. Willy intended to pull in and turn around, nothing more. Driving around aimlessly wasn't going to do him any good, and he was going to have to go home and face his father eventually.

Willy slowed and pulled in, passing by the building where a number of cars had parked. He glided through the parking area and came to a stop behind an old white van with blacked-out windows. It was the one that had taken off the other day when he'd been here with

Reggie. He pulled into the parking space a few places away and got out, thinking he could use the restroom.

Outside, it was quiet, insects and night animals providing a backdrop for the otherwise silent evening. No one seemed to be around, even though cars were there. Willy walked slowly toward the restrooms, trying not to look like he was interested in anything other than the facilities. He thought he might have heard voices from inside the van, but he wasn't sure and didn't investigate or go any closer.

The restroom was empty, which Willy thought very strange. He went into one of the stalls, avoiding the end ones, and peed, thinking for a few seconds. He had a very bad feeling that something not right was going on. Of course, he didn't know what, and he wasn't interested in getting involved. Willy pulled out his phone and brought up the note feature, entering the license number of the van before he forgot it. Then he finished up, washed his hands, and left again, trying to remember as many other license numbers as he could as he went back to his car.

Willy's heart pounded as he got in, locked the door, and entered more license numbers. Then, as he saw a small group of men step out from the side of the building, Willy started the engine, backed out of the spot, and pulled onto the highway back toward town. He didn't stop and barely slowed down until he was parked on the street outside his house. His heart was still racing, and he took deep breaths to calm himself, going over what he'd seen again.

It made no real sense to him, none of it did, and maybe it was nothing, but why would a group of men gather behind the restrooms after dark? Sex was the obvious answer, and maybe that's all it was. But why would one of the guys leave people in the van, then? Was this some sick parent who left his kids in the car while he went to get his jollies?

Willy made a decision. *Reggie, something going on at rest area. Saw same van parked there. Think there were people in it. Group of men behind building. Have license plate numbers.* He sent the text and got an almost immediate answer.

Where are you?

He looked up at the front of the house, his home—at least until his dad found out about him. The lights were on and it seemed warm and inviting. *At home.*

Can you come to the house? I'll have the garage door open and you can pull right in.

Willy read Reggie's message and nearly sent a *no*. With a sigh, he answered *yes* and drove away from his house out toward Reggie's.

There was very little traffic, so it wasn't long before he pulled into Reggie's garage and closed the door. The night air had grown chilly, and he hurried across the yard.

Reggie met him on the porch, holding the door so Willy could go right inside. "What were you doing out there?' Reggie asked as soon as the door closed. Before Willy could stop him, Reggie had tugged him into his arms. "I told you I thought something was going on there."

"Reggie…." Willy tapped his shoulder even as he drank in the heat of his body. "I'm not here for that." He had to be firm. Nothing had changed since this afternoon. He pulled away, even though he wanted to stay in Reggie's embrace. "I was upset and took a drive to clear my head. I wasn't paying attention to where I was going and found myself out there. I went in to use the bathroom, but no one was in there. It was empty. There were cars, but no one was around. That van was in the lot, and I heard voices from inside, I think." He reached into his pocket. "These are the license plates of most of the cars there. The first one is the van."

God, Reggie smelled so good, Willy couldn't help taking a step forward just to get a little more of him, and he shivered. Reggie was in jeans, with a tight T-shirt stretched over his chest. Willy's fingers itched to touch, and he ached to feel the two of them together, to hold him again.

Willy held out his phone and let Reggie take it to jot down the plates. "As I was leaving, a group of men came around the side of the building. I don't know why they were there, and I didn't recognize any of them. They were whispering and talking quickly." That was all Willy knew. "I really need to go. My dad will find out about you

100

because nothing stays quiet in this town, and then...." Willy shrugged and moved toward the door, but Reggie stopped him with a hand on his arm. Willy turned, and Reggie pulled him to him, encircling him in a tight embrace. Reggie kissed him hard and deep, taking his breath away.

"Stay...," Reggie said quietly.

"I can't." Willy wanted to, though. At least for now, as long as they kept quiet, there was a chance for them. But now Willy had to back away and.... His heart ached and burned at the thought. Reggie was temptation come to life. "You made your choice, and I understand it's part of who you are... but I can't...." Tears threatened, and he had to get away before he embarrassed himself completely. "I thought you understood that I needed some time, that I was trying to be independent... that...." He held his breath for a few seconds and released it slowly so he didn't hyperventilate.

"You didn't see his face," Reggie said. "I know I'm the sheriff, but I have a heart, and to see that kid, someone younger than both of us, trying to swim through so much pain and uncertainty. I tried to help him...." He swallowed. "I thought I was being so careful."

"But what you did was make things impossible. Maybe not today, but as soon as Jamie says something, and he will eventually, everyone will know. And that will get to my father fast. He isn't sure about you at all, and whatever doubts he may have will be fueled by this...." Willy took Reggie's hand. "You have to know this town. We're basically simple people, and they understand basic things. They're gossiping like crazy over the mayor's son, and Mayor Fullerton has done a lot for this town. He isn't a jerk or a dummy. He helped get one of the family mills a contract with the state so they could stay in business and continue to employ people. He got the state to repave the highway through town a few years ago so the cars didn't get swallowed up by the potholes. And he's been able to help balance the town budget and make sure the schools have what they need. He's been a dang miracle worker, and yet I've heard people saying he should resign over this." Once Willy started, his words tumbled out and he had little control over them. All his fears welled up, and he tried to keep from giving voice to them, failing miserably. "You know what my father will do."

Reggie gazed at him, head bent forward. "I'm sorry." Seeing Reggie, who usually stood proud and tall, humbled and looking dejected ripped at Willy's heart. He hated him that way.

"Don't. Please. I can take many things, including a beating from my father to protect my brother, but I can't take you looking like that. Sometimes things happen, and we have to hope that something better is going to come along." As soon as the words crossed his lips, Willy doubted he'd meet anyone or anything better than Reggie any time soon.

"There has to be something. I don't want to give you up." Reggie caressed his cheek. "The thought...." He pulled his hand away. "No. I was the one who said that you had more to lose than I did, and I was the one who opened my mouth and pretended that reality didn't exist." He sighed. "I don't know what to do to make it right again."

"You can't put the genie back in the bottle. Not in this town, and not with a juicy piece of information. My father is respected, but he's also feared and even hated by some. And I have to tell you that I don't know what my father will do or how far he'll go if he's honestly and truly challenged. No, I have to back away. I don't have a choice." He sniffed and his leg shook from nerves.

"Willy...," Reggie began.

"Don't you think I want to stay?" Willy demanded. "That I don't want to go back to being alone in a sea of people? Because that's what I am. You... you made me feel less alone and like I might have a place somewhere, with someone. But I was a fool... a stupid kid... to think that somehow things would work out. That I would be able to build some kind of life independent of him so I could separate and go my own way. I want to, but I can't do it at lightning speed, and that's what I'd have to do to be with you now." He swallowed hard. "I've known you for a few weeks.... It seems like longer, but that's all. Am I supposed to turn away from the only life I know, pathetic and lonely as it is, on a whim and a prayer that you won't change your mind? That some... boy will flutter his lonely, sad eyes at you and you'll, what? Give away the keys to the town?" Anger rose in him like a boiling tea kettle, filling the space by the second. He closed his eyes and tried to keep it from spilling over.

"Willy, I'm sorry—"

"I know you are. But you said that you understood and that I could rely on you, and now...."

Reggie hung his head. Of all the things that had happened today, that was probably the worst. "I know. It's my fault. And now both of us have to pay the price. I should have known to keep my mouth shut." Reggie inched closer, and Willy stilled. Reggie didn't stop until his lips pressed to Willy's, stealing his breath. This was a bad idea, and yet he let Reggie hold him tight, even lift him off his feet. Before he could protest, Reggie had him in his arms, carrying him through the house. Reggie set him on the bed. "I am sorry." He kissed him again, and Willy wound his arms around Reggie, clinging to him.

"One more time," Willy said softly, looking into Reggie's eyes. "Is that it?"

"No. I will make this right. Somehow I will undo what I've done." Reggie kissed him, tugging on his lips. "I have to."

"Why?"

"Because this can't be the end. I won't have it. That isn't what I want, and I don't think it's what you want either. So tell me to stop if that's truly what you want, before I go too far." Reggie stilled, not moving, their gazes locked, fire racing up and down Willy's spine. Willy nodded slowly, and Reggie kissed him, pulling at his lips, tongue taking possession of Willy's mouth. Reggie tugged at Willy's clothes, tossing each piece aside when it slipped from his body. The intensity in Reggie's gaze made Willy believe, if only for a while. Reggie slipped off the bed and stripped down to his bare sexiness before stalking back toward him, determination written all over his expression.

"I want you," Reggie whispered.

Willy wanted to ask why once again, but held Reggie closer instead. There were times to question things and other times to take the gifts given and be grateful for them because those gifts wouldn't always be there. The words, or at least the meaning of one of his father's sermons, rattled around in his head, and Willy smiled and then chuckled. "Sorry."

"What's so funny?" Reggie stopped, his hands pressing to Willy's chest, lips just above his. "Am I tickling you?"

"No. It's stupid. I was thinking about one of my father's sermons." Willy rolled his eyes. "See? I said it was dumb." He turned away. "It was one of the things he used to say before…. He doesn't preach that way anymore, but he used to say that we should be thankful for God's blessings and not question them. I was thinking that you were one of those blessings, brought for me, and I…." He sighed. "I needed to stop asking why all the time."

Reggie smiled. "I've never been a religious person, but I think I can agree with that. Whatever God is up there looking over us, I think we should accept his blessings and the good things life gives us. The hardships and difficulties are just around the corner, no matter what we try to do to stop them." Reggie leaned in, nearly closing the distance between them. Then he stilled and didn't move.

Willy blinked, waiting as he decided if he was going to take that advice. It took seconds before Willy crossed the final distance, kissing Reggie and leaning upward to bring them into intimate contact.

Willy loved when Reggie touched him. Correction: Willy loved when Reggie touched him in a way that no one else ever had. Reggie encircled his cock, stroking lightly. Willy thrust his hips into the touch, his eyes crossing. This was amazing and made him feel alive and like he was part of something bigger than just himself. Yeah, it was only a simple touch, Reggie holding him, but for Willy it was so much more than that.

"Damn…." Reggie breathed as air ghosted over Willy's lips. "I do that."

"What?" Willy asked.

Reggie stroked him again, tightening his grip, and Willy arched his back, desperate for more as he gasped and writhed beneath Reggie's solidity. Reggie slithered down his body, his lips and hands trailing behind, making Willy's skin tingle with heated trails that burned all the way to his brain, adding to the building ecstasy. "Make you look and sound…." Reggie gasped. "Like that!" He stroked again.

Willy held Reggie out of fear he was going to fly apart any second. "I can't believe sex feels like this."

Reggie paused, his gaze boring into Willy's. "It can, but it usually doesn't."

"Huh?" Willy blinked, wondering if he'd heard correctly.

"There's sex, and then there's making love. They are different things." Reggie shifted, pulling him even closer, biting his lower lip. "Most parents talk to their kids about sex and how stuff works."

Willy rolled his eyes. "Can you imagine how that conversation happened in my house? My dad sat me down and gave me the Biblical version of what happened between a man and a woman. It was weird beyond belief, and if it hadn't been for the sex education that the state mandated, I would have known next to nothing other than to never, ever, ever do anything, look at anyone, or touch anything until after I was married."

"My parents were a little more helpful. But they always said that you should wait until you loved someone. I've had plenty of sex, but once your heart is involved, everything changes." Reggie leaned closer. "Your heart races just a little bit faster, each touch is amplified, every gaze and breath seems meaningful, and you want more."

"More?" Willy asked.

"Yeah. See, it isn't about needing to come. It's about wanting more. When it's just sex, the payoff is coming. When it's making love, the payoff is in the journey." Reggie released him, placing his hand in the center of his chest. "Being together is what counts, making each other gasp and moan. The shivers that race through you add to my pleasure. Watching your mouth hang open, eyes wide in disbelief and ecstasy. That's what makes it making love. Taking pleasure in the joy of your partner." Reggie's gaze was so intense, Willy could almost feel it physically.

"So this is making love?" Willy asked.

"It is for me," Reggie whispered and swallowed, stroking Willy's cheek with his fingertips. "It was the last time, and that's why I didn't go with you to the motel that night. You deserved to know what this feels like. How good things can be." Reggie shifted, his weight pressing Willy into the mattress. "Every time should be like this for you."

"But how can it be?"

Reggie chuckled. "All you have to do is only go to bed with people your heart is set on. Trust me, lots of sex can be fun, but this… takes your breath away. There is nothing to compare." Reggie lowered his head, lips parting, eyes closing, and Willy held his breath. Reggie kissed him, and the energy he'd been talking about bloomed behind Willy's eyes, spreading through him, fanning out like ripples in a pond. Willy held Reggie tighter, sliding his hands downward to rest in the center of his lower back, pressing them together harder, needing as many points of contact, as much heat and desire, as possible.

"I believe you," Willy gasped as Reggie slid his hands up his thighs and then under him to cup his butt. Willy opened his legs, settling Reggie between them. Thrusting upward, he caught his breath as his cock slid along Reggie's. Within seconds, he understood exactly what Reggie had been trying to tell him. Willy was lost in Reggie's eyes and hoped he was never found again. He could stay in those massive, deep blue eyes, in his strong arms, and against his heated, firm body for the rest of his life.

That wasn't likely to happen, no matter how much Willy might think he wanted it. This, what was between him and Reggie, was an interlude, a last chance, maybe a grasp at happiness. Reality was waiting outside the bedroom door, and it wasn't going to be held at bay forever, no matter how deep and mind-fizzling Reggie's kisses were or how much Willy craved and needed his touch.

"Reggie… I…." Willy held Reggie tighter as Reggie's fingers ghosted over his opening. Willy hadn't been sure he was ready, but lights flashed behind his eyes as he pressed them closed.

"I won't ever hurt you," Reggie whispered, sucking on his ear before doing it again. Willy thought he'd explored what he liked with his own hands in the confines of his bedroom at home, but he'd never imagined what the feel of someone else's fingers and mouth would be like. He shook uncontrollably as Reggie added desire on passion, layering sensation on top of sensation until Willy surrendered to it, giving his pleasure and control to Reggie. Willy let Reggie play him like an instrument and wasn't sorry for a second.

His mind, where thoughts had kept racing in circles like cars on an oval, ground to a halt. Everything, all his attention, centered on Reggie. Nothing else mattered. He pressed forward, holding tightly, snapping his hips as Reggie rolled his, sliding, groaning, adding more.

"Sweetheart," Reggie whispered into his ear. "Settle down just a little." He tugged his hands free and placed them on Willy's chest. "That's it."

"Why?" God, he was back to that.

"Because I want…." Reggie's eyes glinted, and he slid lower, tongue and lips blazing a trail over Willy's chest and belly, down to his….

"Oh God," Willy moaned and did his best to keep his hips still as Reggie's lips closed over his cock, sending him into fits of ecstasy. "You're going to do that again."

Reggie held him, pulling his lips away, grinning. "You like it?" He didn't wait for an answer, gliding his lips downward, taking all of him, encircling Willy in a cave of heat and suction that stole the last of his breath and made his head spin like a top. At first he tried to keep some sort of control on his own body, but soon relinquished it, giving his complete pleasure over to Reggie, and he quickly found he was in the best hands he could ever have possibly imagined. Reggie kept him on the edge, again and again, groaning, writhing, until Reggie took him, shaking, over the mind-blowing edge of passion.

Willy lay still, eyes closed, letting warmth and care wash over him. He was almost afraid to do anything to break this bubble of bliss. It dissipated quickly enough on its own, and he sat up slowly. "I need to...." Willy paused as Reggie grabbed a tissue from the nightstand to clean himself. "Did I do that?" Willy asked, and Reggie smiled, nodding.

"I told you you were sexy." Reggie finished and tossed the tissues in the trash, then lay down next to him, wrapping an arm around Willy's waist.

"I can't stay very long," Willy said, even as he let his eyes drift closed.

"I know." Reggie held him a little tighter. "Still doesn't mean I want you to go." He sighed, and after a few minutes, Willy slowly sat up and climbed out of bed, knowing the longer he stayed, the more tempted he'd be to linger.

Without talking, Willy picked up his clothes and dressed. Reggie sat up, moving to the edge of the bed. Willy did his best not to look at him; otherwise his resolve would crumble, and he really had to go home. He was late as it was and ran the risk of a million questions about where he'd been. Staying out all night was only going to add more, and those were questions he'd like to avoid answering for as long as possible.

"I have to go."

Reggie nodded and tugged him closer, guiding him downward until their lips met. Reggie wound his fingers through his hair, deepening the kiss, and then released him.

Willy stood still, not willing to completely step away from Reggie. "I really have to go." Before his willpower could fade, he turned and left the room, closing the door behind him. He walked as quickly as he could through the house, heading to his car, and backed out of the drive. The loneliness that had been held at bay while he was with Reggie returned with a vengeance in the quiet car interior, and with each passing mile, it grew heavier, culminating as he pulled up in front of his parents' home.

A single porch light burned as Willy quietly went inside. He made as little noise as possible, going to his room and closing the door. It wasn't that late, but his absence was sure to have been noticed and he was going to have to answer for it the following morning. There was little doubt about that.

WHEN WILLY came down for breakfast, his mother set his plate in front of him without a word. "Where's Dad?"

"He went to city hall about something," she answered, turning back to the stove. "I know he's going to want to talk to you."

"I'm sorry I was out late. I lost track of time." His mom would worry, even though he'd been back before eleven.

"Please call next time," she said gently, patting his shoulder.

Willy ate his breakfast, thanked his mom, and went back upstairs to get ready to go to work. He had to be there by nine, and it was just after eight. He had time, but getting out of the house before his father returned was probably a good idea.

As he came down the stairs, he met his father coming up. His father's stern, take-no-prisoners expression stopped him, feet on two different stairs.

"Come. We need to talk." His father turned, and Willy knew what that meant. He was about to get lectured on whatever topic was bothering his father.

Ruthie and Ezekiel bounded down the stairs after him, and thankfully Mom called them into the kitchen for breakfast, so he and his father went into the living room. Willy sat down, running through all the things he'd done in his mind and came up with nothing.

"I understand you were seen last night out by the rest area on the highway." His father leaned forward. "You are never to go out there. That place has a terrible reputation. You know what happened to Jamie Fullerton out there. That place led him to temptation, and I will not have that sort of thing happen to my son." At the vehemence on his father's voice, Willy sat back. "What were you doing out there?"

"I used the bathroom there. That was all. God, Dad. Is this really necessary?" Willy began to stand. He wanted to get the heck out of there as fast as possible.

"Are you sure?"

"Yeah. There was no one else in the building as far as I know, and I did my business, washed my hands, and left."

"Why were you out there?"

Willy shrugged. "I was a little upset and drove out that way to try to think. I realized where I was, used the bathroom, and turned around." He sighed. "I know you have this constant fear about me and everyone else, but this is getting to be a little much. I have my own job now, and I'm an adult. This kind of control you're trying to wield is a little freaky." He had never said anything like this to his father before.

"Freaky!" Man, his father must be upset if he raised his voice. "Because I don't want my son turned into a...."

"What, Dad?" Willy narrowed his eyes, waiting for his father to vocalize his thoughts.

"A sodomite like Jamie," his father finally answered.

Willy shook his head. "What do you think? That someone put something in the water out there that will turn people gay? If that's true, then why don't you just put some antigay in the water at the church?"

His father's cheeks turned scarlet. "Don't you sass me."

"Then make sense," Willy countered quickly. "Maybe actually think before you say something stupid."

The slap stung his left cheek. Willy hadn't even seen it coming. His head snapped to the side, and the sound reverberated off the walls.

Willy turned his head back, staring at his father, meeting his gaze, and then shook his head. "I always knew you were a bully." He stood still, watching as his father leaned back. "I have the scars and now the handprint to prove it." He walked toward the front door, but paused, standing straighter. "I'm going to work. And... yes. I will tell anyone who asks what happened."

"You will not speak to me with that tone!" His father stood and took the few steps to stand in front of him, toe to toe.

"You can ask me things, but I'm your son, not your property. And I don't intend to make a habit of going out the rest area. Like I said, I stopped there to use the bathroom and turn around, nothing more."

Willy breathed deeply. "Now, I need to go to work." He reached for the door and stopped. "Who was it who saw me there?" Willy asked, and his father's expression hardened. "Did it ever occur to you that those people might be the ones who need your help, instead of me? After all, there was no one in the restroom when I was out there, and the only people I saw were coming around from the back of the building. Maybe they are the ones who were out there for something other than a pee." He pulled open the door, stepped outside, and closed it behind him. That should give his father something to think about.

Willy hurried to his car, checked his face in the visor mirror, then started the engine and headed down to work with a slight smile. Maybe Jamie wouldn't say anything about what Reggie had told him and it would be okay to continue to see Reggie. That thought was enough to bring a smile to his lips, at least for now. Willy knew that in this town, few things remained private for long.

CHAPTER 8

REGGIE SMILED at the text message from Willy, asking him to lunch at Sue's Diner just a few doors down from the station.

I have something I have to tell you.

Reggie answered that he could be there in an hour, and after a few minutes' pause, Willy agreed.

An hour later, Reggie found himself sitting in one of the booths right in front, near the windows.

"Why here?" Willy asked from across from him.

"If anyone sees us, they'll never think we're up to something." Reggie smiled, and Willy agreed with a slight nod. "What did you want to tell me?"

"My dad knows who some of the men I saw the rest area are. One of them told him that they saw me out there. Apparently that's the location where hell intersects the earth, at least as far as my dad is concerned. He wouldn't tell me who they were, but I thought you should know in case you wanted to press him." Willy rubbed his cheek slightly and then settled his hands back in his lap. "I wasn't going to try this morning. He and I already had words."

Reggie's anger rose to his throat, and he had to swallow bile as he wondered just how far things had gotten and if more than words had been exchanged. "I don't have to. The one set of plates is registered to someone I've had my eye on for a while." He wasn't going to tell Willy he was looking very closely into why Shawn's personal vehicle had been out there and why he was skulking around behind the building at night. It certainly wasn't for law-enforcement reasons. "One of the other vehicles was registered to James Calder."

Willy narrowed his gaze. "You mean, town councilman James Calder? The owner of the Bank of Sierra Pines and Calder Mill? The one who gave the money to build the library addition?"

"One and the same." Reggie lowered his voice. "You are to tell no one anything. But I bet one of them told your father that he saw you, which means if they are up to no good, that you were seen and recognized. I suspect them telling your dad was a way to warn you off."

"And Dad was at city hall this morning, so I can guess who he spoke with. The Calders are members of Dad's flock. But did you find out where that van was registered?"

Reggie nodded. "The plates are for a 2010 Toyota Corolla owned by Mrs. Claire Fitsimmons of Pasadena. They are obviously stolen plates. I did check her out, and she's seventy-nine years old and no longer owns the car, according to vehicle title records."

Willy chuckled. "You're telling me that those plates belong to a little old lady from Pasadena?"

Reggie put his hands over his mouth and rolled his eyes, wishing he'd made that connection. "Cute. But it really means I'm getting nowhere, other than something is going on out there and it involves a member of the town council." He hated this type of thing. They rarely ended well, and unless he could get solid evidence, it was going to be like walking a minefield.

"What can I get you?" a woman asked as she approached the table.

"Sue, this is Sheriff Reggie Barnett. Sue is an institution, and one of the best cooks in Sierra Pines. Just don't tell my mama I said that."

"My lips are sealed, honey." She smiled and turned to Reggie. "Welcome, Sheriff." She leaned closer. "Can you help me with something? At night I have people hanging around the back door. I don't like it and it makes me nervous for my guys. I told the last sheriff about it and he said he'd do something, but the lazy dingbat never did."

"Of course." Reggie made a call and got through to Jasper. He asked him to make a pass through the rear parking areas. "It's vagrancy, and we need to make sure they move on. Either that or bring them in."

Jasper agreed and said he'd be sure to add it to the patrols.

"Thank you." Sue stood a little straighter. "What can I get you?"

"Chicken salad sandwich with curly fries and some ranch dressing to dip them in," Willy said. That sounded really good, so Reggie ordered the same, with a glass of iced water.

"Hey, Willy," a man said, sliding into the booth next to Willy.

"Hey, Tony," Willy replied. "What are you doing back already?"

"Mom got sick and Dad needed some help, so I came back for a few days. They're running some tests. She should be okay. They think it's nerves, but they want to be sure." Tony looked at Reggie. "Is Willy in trouble or something?"

"No." Willy giggled. "This is Sheriff Barnett. He and I have met a couple times and have gotten to be friends."

Reggie extended his hand, and Tony shook it.

"I don't want to interrupt your lunch, but I saw you and had to stop in to say hi." Tony slid out of the booth again. "See ya later." He hurried to the counter, where he paid for an order and took it to go, waving before disappearing out the door.

"He's something," Reggie said.

"Nothing stops Tony. He's trying to break into the movies, and I hope it goes well for him. But I think he has more hopes than prospects. That's okay, though. He's a nice guy, and I see him when he comes to town." Willy slid back over until he was in the center of the booth seat once again.

Their conversation grew quiet, but Willy gazed at him, a goofy expression on his face. Reggie couldn't help smiling. It was obvious to him what Willy was thinking, and it was both flattering and dangerous. They were in public, and Willy was looking at him like he was the center of the universe. Not that there was anything wrong with that, and Reggie was more than flattered. He loved that Willy thought of him that way, but to have those feelings so brazenly naked on his face—that could be dangerous for them. Still, Reggie didn't want to do anything that would hurt Willy.

"How is work going?" Reggie was banking on changing the subject to something mundane, and it worked.

114

"Really busy. Mr. Webster seems happy with the job I'm doing, and I work hard. I want him to like me and keep me around. I also saw a posting on one of the message boards in the store for an apartment, so I thought I'd take a look at it. But I'm not sure I can afford that much rent yet. Still, I need to look."

It constantly surprised him how mature Willy was. He didn't whine or cry "poor me" about his situation. Willy made a plan and did his best to stick to it. "That's really good, but don't rush into anything you don't have to."

"I won't, but...." Willy paled as his gaze shifted over Reggie's shoulder. Reggie turned, following it as Reverend Gabriel barreled through the door of the diner and up to their table.

"What are you doing here with... him?" The anger rolled off him, eyes blazing with righteous indignation. "What are you trying to do to my son?" he demanded, turning his vehemence on Reggie.

"I think you need to cool down." Reggie reached to his hip, ready to protect himself and Willy if necessary. "Remember where you are and who you're speaking to." He kept the volume level, but let a growl of caution enter his voice. "I am not doing anything to your son. I'm the sheriff of this town, and any threat will be met with the force necessary to protect myself and him. Do you understand?"

"I don't care who you are or why you decided to become 'friends' with my son. I will not have your kind of influence on him. I don't know what you did to Jamie Fullerton, but you somehow got to him and corrupted him with your—"

"Please," Willy said, sliding out of the booth to stand next to his father. "This is not the place."

"Listen to your son," Reggie echoed, sliding out of the booth as well. All eyes in the restaurant were on them. Reggie could feel the curiosity in multiple gazes pointed in their direction. He reached to his wallet, got out a twenty and a five, and left them on the table before motioning toward the front door. He needed to diffuse this situation before it escalated out of control. At least that's what his police training told him. His heart felt as though the floor had dropped away. This was exactly what Willy had been warning him about.

115

He waited for Reverend Gabriel to leave before motioning to Willy and then following where he could keep an eye on everyone.

"How dare you come here," Reverend Gabriel began as soon as the door swung closed. "How dare you bring your kind—" His lips turned up into a sneer. "—into this town... my town."

"First thing, Reverend, this isn't your town. You live and work here, the same as everyone else. Now, why don't you tell me what has you so upset?" Reggie gentled his voice and played innocent.

"Don't go there. It's all over town that you're gay and that you've been seen with my son and are trying to recruit him... or whatever it is you do."

Reggie stepped back to avoid a flood of spittle as Reverend Gabriel pulled Willy to stand next to him.

"Reggie is my friend," Willy said with a strength and calmness that made Reggie's heart warm. "He's a good man, and you need to stop this." Willy looked up and down the sidewalk to where people were stopping to watch.

"He's a sodomite, and I will not have you spending time with people like that. I will *not* have it. Now, come with me—you're going home." He grabbed Willy's arm, but Willy wrenched himself away. Reggie saw that self-centered, "I rule the family" attitude that Willy had described to him.

"I'm on my lunch break, and I'm going back to work." Willy stepped back and then turned to walk down the sidewalk toward the drugstore.

Relief flooded Reggie that Willy had extricated himself from this situation.

"As for you...." Reverend Gabriel's chest heaved and the fire in his eyes grew more intense. If this had been a movie, they might have glowed red. "You will stay away from my son, and you will—"

"Stop!" Reggie barked. "You never issue me orders. I am the sheriff of this town, and you are not my boss." He stepped forward, puffing out his chest. "Just stop, or I will have you arrested and charged with threatening a police officer." That let the wind out of Reverend Gabriel's sails almost immediately, and Reggie lowered his

116

voice. He needed to calm this situation. "Your son is an adult, and he's perfectly capable of making his own decisions regarding his life and how he wishes to spend his time." Even as he said the words, Reggie regretted that he'd brought this turmoil into Willy's life. Images flashed through his head of the hardness and efforts to control him that were going to close over Willy like a cage on his young soul. And this was all his fault. "I think you should go home and give yourself some time to think before you do something you're going to come to regret."

Reverend Gabriel's posture slumped slightly. "You need to stay away from Willy. I will not have you leading him astray. And as for you being the sheriff, I intend to see to it that we make that position as temporary as possible."

Reggie smiled briefly, shook his head, and decided he'd had enough of this. "You have a nice day." He stepped back and waited for the shocked reverend to turn away. Reggie had been right. Reverend Gabriel was not used to being dismissed, and that threw him. He was truly a bully of sorts, and once his threat and bluster were ignored, he lost his power. It was clear that there was nothing Reggie could do at the moment other than step back, diffuse some of the emotion that had charged through the exchange, and bring this to an end. He was not going to be able to change what Reverend Gabriel thought in the next five minutes.

As much as he liked his job and wanted to keep it, he was much more concerned about Willy and how he was going to take the brunt of his father's anger at some point. That worried him, especially as Reggie watched Willy's father march down the sidewalk. This had the potential to go very badly, and there was nothing Reggie could do to stop it.

"Is it true?" Sam asked as he came into Reggie's office, with Jasper on his heels. "Wow, a gay sheriff in Sierra Pines," Sam added once Reggie nodded. There was no need to keep things quiet.

"Yes. I'm gay. But that doesn't affect the job we all have to do."

"It shouldn't, no," Jasper agreed, biting his lower lip. "For the record it doesn't matter to me if you're gay. You've been good to work for." That sounded suspiciously ominous.

"What does that mean?" Sam asked.

Jasper sighed and shrugged. "You know Reverend Gabriel and the council are going to have a fit. A gay sheriff in Sierra Pines, this town where they all hold us as some sort of California bastion of family values." He rolled his eyes and turned to Reggie. "I think you're a great sheriff and I don't care if you're gay or not. Doesn't matter to me." Jasper turned to go. "I'm going out to patrol."

"Be safe," Reggie said, and Jasper smiled and left the office.

"Shawn is going to have a field day with this," Sam told him. He was clear-eyed and had been for days now. The scent of alcohol was also conspicuously absent. "I don't want him as sheriff. He'd make a terrible one. Shawn doesn't give a crap about the department or anyone around him. All he wants is to be sheriff and have the power that goes along with it." He shook his head. "There will be people who will make a lot of noise about this, but there are also plenty of people in this town who aren't going to care if you're gay or not, as long as you do your job and protect them."

Reggie hadn't expected to find support from Sam. It was a surprise.

"Thanks, Sam." Reggie nodded. "I know who I am, and if people accept me or not…." He shrugged. "I'm going to continue to do my job. That's what I'm here for. The reverend and the council can do what they like, but they have little power over us or the department." He smiled quickly, and Sam nodded and turned to leave the office.

"I'm patrolling the north side. Is there anything I should be aware of?"

"Just make a pass down the area behind Sue's when you can. She's reported vagrants."

"No problem." Sam left the office as well, and Reggie sat back in his chair, the dang thing squeaking as he did. He had plenty of work to do and needed to get busy, but damn it all, he worried about Willy.

Reggie snatched his phone and sent him a text to make sure he was okay. He waited for an answer and received one an hour later. Reggie had no idea what else he could do. Now everything was up to Willy and what he decided he wanted.

Reggie had made a real mess of everything. He should have stuck to his own rules and none of this would have happened. He wouldn't be sitting at work worrying about Willy so much that his leg shook, and he wouldn't be in the position of wondering how badly he was going to have to fight to keep his job. He had the support, it seemed, of two of his deputies, and that was more than he'd expected. Still, he could get another job and move on if he had to. It was Willy he was truly worried about. It seemed as though the worst that could happen was coming to pass. He could take finding another job or fighting for the one he had, but the thought of not seeing Willy again left him cold—glacially, arcticly cold—and Reggie wondered if he'd ever be warm again.

CHAPTER 9

WILLY SAT in the office of the store, finishing up his day's work, and then closed the application and locked the computer. He dreaded going home.

"Willy," Mr. Webster said as he came in and sat down in the other chair. "I think you and I might need to talk."

"Yes, sir."

"There are rumors going through town about the sheriff and, well... I've seen the two of you together."

Willy tried to stifle the gasp, but he failed.

"That's what I thought."

"I-I...," Willy stammered and grew quiet.

"You have nothing to be ashamed of," Mr. Webster said, and leaned forward. "I'm not going to fire you or anything like that." He ran his fingers nervously over his partially bald head. "There's going to be grief headed his way, and you know it."

"Yeah, I do." Willy was well aware of the shitstorm that was about to hit.

"Is that because you're afraid for Reggie, or for yourself?" Mr. Webster's gaze fell on Willy's shaking hands. "You're still young and have your whole life ahead of you. But the one you have will depend on the choices you make and the kind of person you decide you want to be. I already know you're conscientious and a hard worker...."

"I don't know what you mean."

Mr. Webster nodded. "Of course you don't. I've lived in this town most of my life. I left to go to pharmacy school, and I intended to head out to the big city, open my own place, maybe start a chain like CVS. Then my mom got ill and my dad said he needed help, so I put that on hold and returned. I never left again. I stayed and took care of my parents. Eventually I got married and had kids, like everyone expected me to." He sighed softly. "I sometimes wonder how my life would have been different if I hadn't come back."

"So I should...?" Willy trailed off, unsure what he wanted to ask.

"I had big plans, but there came a point where I had to ask myself what I truly wanted. It sounds like an easy question, but it isn't." Mr. Webster clapped him on the knee and pulled back his hand. "I've known your dad for a long time. I bet you didn't know that he and I went to high school together and were friends of a sort. Your dad was a very different person then. Wild, crazy, and the center of fun. But he changed as he grew older, like we all did. After your brother died, he changed again, and not for the better, in my opinion. He's all about controlling everything and everyone he can so he doesn't have to repeat the pain and loss he went through when Isaac died."

"I know that. I can remember those times." God, he longed for them so much. He wanted his dad back. But his dad had died along with Isaac, and all he had was a father now.

"Your dad wants to choose the kind of person you'll be, but he doesn't have that right unless you give it to him. Am I making any sense at all?" Mr. Webster asked.

"I think so."

"Deciding what you want seems like such an easy thing to do. You picture it, say what you want, and then go get it. But it doesn't work that way. Sometimes you have to fight for it, and sometimes what you really want isn't what you thought at the beginning. See, I thought I wanted a chain of stores and to become rich, the head of an empire. But I came back here, helped my family, met my wife, and she changed my life. She showed me that what I truly wanted, soul-deep, was a life with her. I started working here, bought the place from the previous owner, eventually remodeled and changed the name, and now it's part of my life."

"I think I understand," Willy said with a smile.

"I doubt it. Because it took me years to understand, fully. I didn't sit down to make any grand decision. I went with the wind and my heart. All that was at stake for me was my old dream. One path opened up to me, and I took it. The other path closed, eventually. And that's fine. My parents and friends supported me."

Willy nodded. "I need to decide who I want to be and what my own path will look like."

"Yes. But your path is going to change the paths of a lot of other people. It will affect your brother and sister, your mom and dad, yourself, as well as that of a certain sheriff who can't seem to take his eyes off you whenever the two of you are in the same room." Mr. Webster smiled at him, and Willy's burden became a little lighter.

"What do I do?" Willy asked.

Mr. Webster shook his head. "I don't know. That isn't for me to say. This is one of those times when you have to make your own choices. Your father runs your family like he's some kind of king. He makes the rules, and the rest of you follow along. If you let him, your dad will make all the decisions for you for the rest of your life."

"Tell me about it," Willy groused.

"My dad used to say that there comes a time in everyone's life, man or woman, where you have to choose the kind of life you want. I think this may be one of those times for you." Mr. Webster patted his knee once again. "Just make sure that whatever you do, it's the right thing for you."

Willy nodded. "But what if…?" He closed his eyes, knowing no decision would come without a cost. He knew how his father was going to react, and when he got home, he was going to have to face the music. Mr. Webster was correct: Willy was going to have to make decisions, and how he did that was going to decide the man he was going to be. "Thank you."

"It's no problem. I had the same talk with my son last year. He had the chance to go to school out east, but he was afraid to move that far away. That kind of change can be hard for people. Robin and his mother were always very close, and after the cancer scare from a few years ago, it was very difficult for him. But he decided to go and is doing very well at Yale. He loves it now, and I doubt he'll ever come back here to live again. And that's okay. He needs to find his own way, just like you do."

"Yeah, but your son isn't gay and you didn't throw him out of the house because of it." Willy stared at the floor.

"Robin isn't gay, but he did surprise his mother and me when he brought home his latest girlfriend. She's from India, and it was a bit of a shock. It didn't take long for Cheryl and me to get over it. Though I understand that Prima's parents still haven't come around to the fact that she's in love with a non-Indian boy." Mr. Webster chuckled a little. "We have met them, and I think that went a long way to smoothing things over for them." He shrugged. "Parents don't always like what their children want. But you can't live your life for your father any more than Prima could live her life for hers. It took guts on her part to stand up to them."

Willy nodded slowly. "Thanks." It was going to take all the courage he possessed in every fiber of his being to be able to deal with his father. "I appreciate you taking the time to talk to me. Sometimes it's easy to think you're all alone."

"You aren't." Mr. Webster smiled and left the office.

Willy turned back to make sure everything had been put away before leaving as well. He didn't want to go home and thought about wandering down to the police station to see if Reggie was there. But then he figured it was best if he didn't give his father much more ammunition, at least right now.

WILLY STOOD outside the house an hour later, once again very much alone. He knew his father was inside and his mother was most likely in the kitchen, but while she might be understanding or even sympathetic, but she wasn't going to take his side against his father. He wished Reggie was with him. Without thinking, he turned in the direction of the sheriff's station and smiled. Maybe he was here. Willy didn't need Reggie standing next to him in order to be able to channel his strength.

Willy marched up the walk and went inside. Immediately the scent of his mother's pot roast, potatoes, and carrots wrapped around his senses. The warmth dissipated as his father stepped in front of him.

"What have you to say for yourself?"

"About what?" Willy crossed his own arms in front of his chest, mirroring what he'd seen Reggie do, drawing himself to his full height.

"You need to be more careful when you pick your friends. And I expect you to stay away from him. I've already had a talk with a number of council members, and—"

"What? You expect to browbeat them into breaking the law?" Willy felt as though Reggie were standing right behind him. "Maybe you should bring your attitudes out of the Stone Age and into the twenty-first century. Reggie is a good sheriff, and you're going to find a number of business owners in this town who like him. The council and you will get feedback if you don't back off this witch hunt. You are free to believe what you wish, as is every man and woman in this town, including me." He did his best to stop his knees from knocking.

"I will not have that kind of—"

Willy cut him off. "What? *Logic* in your house? Maybe a little compassion and feeling?" He spoke fast, emotions rising. "What happened to my dad? He's gone and has been since Isaac was killed. All I have left is a father, a person I don't like very much. He's strict, stuffy, no fun, and certainly not someone I want to be around. I want my dad back." Willy lowered his arms as his father slowly rocked back and forth. "I want the man who used to take me fishing and went camping with us. The one who used to read us stories... ones that didn't always come from the Bible. I want the dad who used to take us out for ice cream on the nights that Mom went to Ladies Aid, and we weren't supposed to tell her." God, he remembered having fun with him. "I miss the Saturdays when you, me, and Isaac used to go hiking up in the mountains. You'd work on your sermon sometimes, preaching to the trees at the top of your voice. Isaac and I would giggle as the words echoed back, occasionally sounding dirty." He sighed and shrugged. "Do you remember teaching Isaac how to drive? Taking us into the mountains and letting me drive the car when I wasn't supposed to?"

"Isaac is dead," his father said flatly. "And he isn't coming back."

"Yes. Isaac is gone. But the rest of us aren't, though sometimes you act like everything good died along with him. It didn't. The rest of us are still here." Willy reached out, taking one of his dad's hands. "I just want my dad back," he whispered, then released his hand and walked past his stunned father and on into the kitchen, where his mother stared at him in near shock.

"That wasn't what I wanted to talk about," his father said, coming in behind him.

"But Willy is right," his mother said. "We've been living in a daze of grief for years, and you've become unbearable." She slammed the spoon she'd been using on the counter. "I don't want to live like this anymore. I want to be happy again, and I don't know how." She leaned over the sink, and his father reached up to her shoulders. She turned, and he held her. That was the last Willy saw as he quietly left the kitchen to go upstairs to his room. Closing the door, he leaned against it and nearly slid to a seated position as he thought of what he'd just done.

"Willy?" Ezekiel asked from the other side of the door, nearly in tears. Willy got to his feet, opened the door, and lifted him into his arms. "Why is Mama crying?"

"Because she's sad. But it's okay, I think."

"Where's Daddy?" He sniffled.

"With Mommy."

Ezekiel rested his head on Willy's shoulder. "Are we gonna have dinner?"

"Yes. Just stay here for a little while, and then we'll go down for dinner." Willy needed to give them time to talk. His mother speaking up, at least in front of any of the kids, was something he could barely remember. Willy held Ezekiel a few minutes and then carried him down the stairs.

Willy almost didn't know how to act as his dad and mom brought the food to the table. He set Ezekiel at his place and called Ruthie to dinner. Neither of them seemed to understand quite how to act either.

They looked back and forth between their mom and dad as the two of them talked to each other at dinner.

"What did you do today, Mom?" Willy asked.

"I worked with some of the new moms. They asked to meet with me. I love being around all the babies." His mom smiled, and like that, some of the tension that seemed to have hung over their lives lessened. Even his father's eyes seemed a little brighter than they had been for years.

Willy had no illusions that things were going to change for him that easily. But who knew? Maybe his mother would influence his father.

"You and I still need to talk," his father said after a while, as his mother filled plates and they were passed around. Of course, Willy shouldn't have expected that he'd deflected his father away from what he wanted, at least not permanently.

"I think we've talked about enough for tonight," his mother said. "Unless William has something he wishes to talk to you about, let it go." She continued dishing up, but the pronouncement was clear. His father met her gaze, but she didn't back down. "I'm tired of mourning. Isaac is gone. It was an accident, and we need to start living again, all of it… for the sake of the kids. And if you aren't going to do that, then I'll figure out a way to do it on my own." She plopped a plate in front of his father, and Willy realized just how big a kettle of worms he'd opened.

"Rachel," his father said with more real emotion and tenderness than Willy had heard from him in a long time.

"I mean it, Gabriel. This has gone on long enough. The cold, the just existing—we deserve more than that. The kids need to be in a house that's alive and happy. It hasn't been, not in a long time. And I want something more."

Willy ate and let his parents talk. "It's okay," Willy told Ezekiel when he tugged on his sleeve.

Ezekiel clearly wasn't so sure. "Daddy will be mad," he said. "He scares me."

126

Willy put an arm around him and caught the shock on his father's face.

Ezekiel ate slowly, alternating his gaze between their mother and father. Willy ate as well, while Ruthie shoveled her food into her mouth and then asked to be excused, exiting the room before she got an answer.

"The kids don't even know how to understand the two of us talking. You've made pronouncements and set rules, and I've said nothing, but that's over. I can't keep living like this."

"Rachel, I…." His father seemed to have been rocked deeply. It wasn't often that Willy saw him speechless, but he seemed to be now.

"Willy is old enough to decide who he wants his friends to be. He doesn't need your interference and self-righteous preaching." She stood, pushing her chair back. "Gabriel, you don't know everything, and Willy is capable of building his own life and making his own decisions and mistakes. Lord knows you made plenty of them in your day." She turned to Ezekiel and gently patted his arm. "Go ahead and eat, honey. Everything is okay." Then she left the room, and Willy stared at his father, whose mouth hung open.

"You know, Dad, I guess now isn't really the time to tell you I'm gay, but I'm going to anyway." Willy went back to eating as his father slumped in his chair.

"Is that a joke? Because it certainly isn't funny," his father growled.

"No, Dad. It's not a joke. I'm as gay as Jamie Fullerton, and I'm tired of hiding who I am from you and everyone else. I've been afraid of you for years, but I'm not going to live that way anymore. I am who I am, and I have someone in my life who I care about, though I came *this close* to walking away from him because of you." Willy set down his fork. "I told you I wanted my dad back. If I still had him, I could have talked to him and told him about the hard time I was having for the last few years, but my father…. Him I can't talk to. He's exactly what Mom said, a self-righteous pain in the ass." Willy pushed back his chair. "I always thought that as soon as you found out, you'd kick me out of the family. But I don't care anymore. I want to be happy, just like Mom, and I can't do that here… with you." Willy left the room, heading for the stairs.

"Where are you going?"

"Upstairs to pack my things. I have no idea where I'm going to go, but I won't live the life you want just to try to make you happy." Willy took the first steps upward and felt a hell of a lot better with each step he took. He had to make his own way.

His father didn't yell or come after him, but he didn't call out to stop Willy either.

Willy went to his room and pulled his old suitcase out from under the bed. He quickly packed it, then grabbed his laptop and slipped it into his backpack. It took him ten minutes to pack what was important to him. He sat on the edge of the bed, wondering what he was going to do. Then he picked up the phone.

CHAPTER 10

REGGIE SAT in his patrol car, heading south out to the scene of an accident. The fire department was already en route, and initial reports were multiple injuries and possible fatalities. As he approached, the scope of the accident became apparent. A white van lay on its side, with a delivery truck parked by the side of the road, its front end ripped up.

"It was an accident! They didn't even have their headlights on," the driver was saying over and over again as Reggie approached him. "It veered into my lane, and I couldn't get out of the way."

"I understand. Please stay with your vehicle. I'll be back to speak with you in a minute."

"Once it rolled over, the back door opened and four or five people got out." The delivery driver leaned against the side of his truck.

Reggie motioned to ambulance personnel, and they hurried over to help him. Jasper arrived seconds later, and Reggie got him managing traffic, because as soon as word of the accident got out, people would file by to see what was going on.

"How is the driver?" Reggie asked as rescue workers got him out of the van.

Firefighters shook their heads as EMTs loaded the man into an ambulance and then left without their siren, a clear sign that he was already dead.

Reggie's phone vibrated in his pocket, and he pulled it out. "Oh no," he said under his breath as he read Willy's message. *I'm working an accident. Go to the house and I'll be there as soon as I can*, he sent in return.

"You'll want to look at this," Howard, the fire chief, told him. "There was no one else in the van when we started work." He motioned toward the back of the van, and Reggie peered into the open doors.

Blankets were strewn everywhere, a cooler had been flung to the side of the road, with ice and bottles of water everywhere, and shoes and items of women's clothing littered the ground.

Reggie knelt down, examining one of the blankets. "That looks like blood." He went back to his car and returned with an evidence kit, gathering everything he could find.

"There's more blood over here," Howard said, pointing toward the tree line. "Someone else was injured." A few drops of blood led to the trees.

One of the firefighters agreed to switch with Jasper, and Reggie pulled him from traffic control. "Protect the scene, I'll be right back." Reggie followed the trail of blood into the trees, using his flashlight to shine the way. He didn't get very far. The blood trail ended after a few steps. The woods were thick, and it was well after dark. This wasn't the movies, and a search at this time of day was only going to lead to others getting hurt. "Is anyone in there?" he called. "We're here to help." Reggie waited for any sort of response, then called again.

"Why would they just take off?" Jasper asked when Reggie joined him again.

"Because they're scared. And maybe none of them are supposed to be here." Reggie tagged the bloody fabric as evidence and slowly went through what had been the contents of the van. He found very little that was personal until he widened the search. A bag had been thrown from the van and had ended up forty or fifty feet from the scene. Inside were clothes and a small prayer book in Spanish. "Jesus," Reggie said under his breath. "No wonder they took off, even injured. They were scared to be seen by anyone."

"I don't understand," Jasper said.

"Tag this and get it into evidence, and then secure the van with everything inside. Have it hauled to the station. We need to go through everything in it." That was going to take hours. It was time he started using his people. "Call Sam and get him in, then take charge of the car when it arrives."

"On it." Jasper hurried away, practically bouncing.

Reggie shook his head, walking back to the ambulance, where the truck driver sat with a blanket over his shoulders. "Are you okay? What's your name?"

"Jack Parnell. They said it was shock, but I'm okay."

"Tell me about the accident," Reggie said.

"It was dark, and they were coming up from the south. There were no lights, and by the time I saw them... I jammed on the brakes and clipped the driver's side. The van twisted around and then rolled on its side. I pulled off right away, and after a minute, the back doors opened and five people got out. I asked if they were okay. They spoke Spanish, and one was hurt, but they helped him and grabbed bags and ran for the trees. I don't think they could have been hurt too badly, but they were just gone. I suppose it was a miracle and all." He hung his head. "I didn't mean to hurt anyone, but I never saw them."

Reggie took notes, making sure he got all the personal information.

"The driver's dead, isn't he?" he asked, and Reggie nodded. "I thought so. That part took the brunt. I suppose I should be relieved no one else was injured. Were those people just riding loose in back?"

"I don't think so. There were seats. My guess is that they were buckled in. We'll know more once we get it back for investigation. But are you sure you're okay?"

He nodded slowly. "Yes. The truck was damaged and I got a little banged up, but that was all." He took a deep breath. "Why didn't they have their lights on? I would have seen them and could have gotten out of the way. They were over the center line, and I didn't have much time to react."

Reggie detected no indication of subterfuge or anything other than absolute truthfulness and regret. "Thank you."

"Can I call someone to pick me up?" the truck driver asked.

"Of course," Reggie answered. "Can we do anything to help? We can have the truck towed."

"I called my company, and they were going to do that. I just wasn't sure how much longer you would need me." He hung his head.

"I can contact you if I need anything more. Call your friends or family." Reggie turned, watching as everyone worked. The back door of the van had been closed, and Jasper stood guard as the wrecker loaded it on the back. That was one job done, and soon enough the second tow truck arrived and took care of the truck. Bit by bit the scene was cleared away. Jasper followed the van back to the station, and Reggie made sure the last details were handled before leaving the now-empty scene.

REGGIE TIED things up at the station, making sure all evidence was secured, and then went home. The house was dark when he arrived, and Reggie wondered if Willy was going to be there. He went inside and found Willy curled up on the sofa under the throw he kept on the back, the television on low. Reggie quietly left the room to put his gun away before returning.

"Hey," Reggie said, sitting carefully on the edge of the sofa. "What happened?" He gently rubbed Willy's back, thrilled that he was there.

Willy slowly rolled over, blinking at him. "Well, I told my father. I'm not hiding anymore. We had one of the weirdest conversations I think I can ever remember, and then my mom started in on him. That part was pretty unexpected. Then I told him, because... I don't want to spend my life lying. I know my dad doesn't approve of me, but at least he knows who I am now." Willy yawned.

"Are you really okay?" Reggie slid closer, impressed and proud. "That's a lot to go through."

"I think I am. My dad didn't yell or anything—I think he was too off-balance to do that."

"What did he say?"

Willy shook his head. "Nothing. I just left the house. He didn't stop me, and neither did my mom. My dad was upset that I was friends with you." He sighed. "Things have been pretty bad at home for a long time. I told him about how I wasn't happy and that I wanted my dad back." Willy sat up, and Reggie hugged him. "It was pretty surreal. I don't think I've ever seen my dad speechless."

"I was really worried when you texted," Reggie said.

"I wasn't sure where to go. I know my dad didn't order me to get out of the house, but I couldn't stay." Willy leaned against him, and Reggie put his arms around him. "I guess I was hoping you'd understand."

"I do." But Reggie also didn't want Willy to give up on his family.

"Did you get something to eat? What time is it?" Willy yawned. "I'm sorry I fell asleep." He reached for his phone from the coffee table. "Nothing. I guess I was hoping someone might call."

Reggie couldn't blame Willy. "Give them a little time. Your dad is going to have a lot to process, based on what you told me." Reggie's stomach rumbled, and Willy jumped to his feet, hurrying to the refrigerator.

"I made some pasta and sauce. I'll heat some of it up for you. I wasn't expecting you to be so late. It must have been really bad." He pulled out a plate and placed it in the microwave.

"It was. But I think I have a better idea about what's been going on in town. You said that when you saw that white van, you thought you heard voices, right?" Reggie asked.

"Yeah." Willy got a beer and brought it over to him, and when the microwave beeped, he hurried back and brought over a plate of pasta that smelled rich and savory, with mouthwatering garlic and oregano. He handed it to Reggie and sat next to him on the sofa. "Like multiple people talking very quietly. I couldn't understand what they were saying."

Reggie took a bite, humming softly. "Do you think that was because they weren't speaking English?"

Willy paused and snuggled a little closer. "Possibly. It was hard for me to tell. Like I said, I couldn't really understand them, and then this group of men came from behind the building. Why?"

Reggie took another bite and swallowed. "There was an accident tonight. A van was hit and rolled onto its side. The other driver said five people got out of the back of the van. They seemed shaken up but hurried into the woods. There was a trail, but it was too late to follow it. I'll try in the morning when there's some light, but I doubt I'm going to find anything."

"Why? What are you thinking?"

"Human trafficking of some kind. People being transported illegally. I'm not sure what the purpose of the people here was. There may have been people who paid to get them across the border from Canada and then down to San Francisco or Los Angeles. It's out of the way here, and it isn't likely this route is going to be watched as much as the more major routes."

"Is that what you think was going on out at the rest area?" Willy asked.

Reggie nodded, taking another bite and groaning. The pasta tasted damn good, and he was suddenly famished. "Think about it." He continued eating, the need for food overwhelming almost everything else. "They would need a place to conduct business.... Maybe someone paving the way so they don't get stopped or questioned." The more he thought about it, the more he realized that this could be what Shawn was up to. Reggie set the plate on the table, his hands curling into fists. If that were true, Reggie was going to hang the bastard by his balls. "I saw a documentary on National Geographic about it. They use out-of-the-way places. They have to have safe areas to refuel and let people out, things like that. The rest area would be good for them. It's relatively isolated, and with someone running interference for them, they can feel safe and pass right through without anyone questioning it."

"Yeah, but now won't they change their routes? There's been an accident, and they have to know that one of their vans is in custody. They can't continue to use this route, so they'll go somewhere else."

Reggie couldn't argue with that logic. "Maybe. They have to have put a lot of resources into building whatever organization they have, though. They aren't going to abandon it just like that. They may back off, but they'll return as soon as they think the heat is off." He was already thinking of ways to help ensure that's what they thought. He tugged Willy closer. "Right now, I'm more concerned about you and your father. Are you really going to be okay?"

"I don't know," Willy said. "I had to get out of the house and away from him for a while. And you were the first person I thought

about contacting, but I don't know where I'm going to go from here."
Willy shrugged. "I have what I could take with me in my car, and that's
pretty much all of it." He turned and leaned against him, burying his
face in Reggie's shirt.

"Sweetheart, don't worry. You can stay here as long as you need
to." Reggie wanted to move Willy into his bedroom and not let him
go. Reggie leaned closer, burying his nose in Willy's hair, inhaling
deeply. He might have been crying. Reggie wasn't sure and wasn't
going to ask. Sometimes a guy might need to cry, but he didn't need
to be called out for it. Reggie simply held him, soaking in the heat as
he clung to him.

"I don't know what's going to happen. I know that once my
father gets his emotional feet under him again, he's going to be mad
as a wet hen, and he'll come after you."

Reggie tightened his hug. "I'm a big boy. I can take whatever
your father or the rest of this damn town wants to throw at me. I'm
tired of hiding just to please other people. I am who I am…." He tilted
Willy's chin upward. "And you are who you are." He smiled. "And I
can't tell you how proud I am. Willy, you have to be the gutsiest man
I've ever met."

Willy shook his head. "Have you ever been shot at?" Willy
asked. It seemed like a strange question at the moment, but Reggie
answered with a nod. "Did you wet yourself or run the other way?"

"No. I took cover and wounded the shooter so he could be
arrested."

"See, that's courage. All I did was open my big mouth." Willy
closed his eyes and leaned against him once more. "I got tired of my
father running my life, and I just told him."

Reggie humphed. "What you did was tell your father and your
family who you really are. It was like being naked in front of them.
You exposed the person inside and said to hell with them if they
didn't like what they saw. That's the real courage in life. It isn't about
being shot at. Bravery is easy. It only takes a few seconds to be brave
and handle a situation. Bravery is momentary and comes in spurts—
courage comes from inside and allows us to be who we are." Reggie

tipped Willy's face upward, leaned closer, and kissed him. "Courage is also the sexiest thing in the world." He deepened the kiss, heat rising like a geyser from the base of his spine.

Willy wound his arms around Reggie's neck, holding them together, returning the kiss, echoing back every ounce of energy Reggie sent to him. "I want you, Reggie," Willy whispered, and when Reggie pulled back, a tear ran down Willy's cheek. "I thought... I thought I could just walk away and go back to the way things were. That I could be with you one last time and then have the life I had before. But I can't. See, you were there—you just didn't know it."

"I don't understand." The words were rough as Reggie spoke around the grapefruit in his throat.

"When I told my dad, you were there with me, standing next to me. I could feel you. I carried you along with me to help me be brave." Willy gasped and spoke faster and faster. "My dad and I were talking. Well, I did the talking this time, and I was so tired of the way things were. I told him everything I felt, and then afterward, I just continued. And when he started in on you, I told him I was gay and that maybe he didn't know as much as he thought he did. But you were there with me, right beside me. I could almost feel you."

"Did you do that for me?" Reggie asked in near horror. He had no illusions that such an admission was going to come without repercussions, and the thought that Willy could be hurt because of something he'd done for him.... The lump in Reggie's throat expanded further.

"No. I did it because I figured out the kind of man I wanted to be. See, I wanted to be the man who was good enough and strong enough to be your boyfriend. I wanted to be someone I could be proud of, to hold my head high, and I wanted to be good enough for you." Another tear ran down Willy's cheek.

"Sweetheart, you were good enough for me the very day you were born." Reggie crashed his lips onto Willy's, tasting him, needing more and not able to get it no matter what he did. "What I keep wondering is what I ever did to deserve you."

"Me?"

Reggie nodded, his thumb ghosting over Willy's lower lip, the heat tingling the pad of his finger. "I'm older than you, and I've seen the best and worst of humanity in my job, but you take my breath away. Your strength and...." He couldn't talk any longer. Instead, Reggie stood and held out his hand to help Willy to his feet. Reggie turned out the lights and left everything where it was as he led Willy down the hall. He paused briefly at the guest room, continued on to his, and pushed the door open with his foot. As he entered the room, he lifted Willy into his arms.

Their lips came together in a blinding flash of joy and passion that threatened to overwhelm Reggie completely, carrying off his soul. He lowered Willy to the bed and slowly stepped back. "I love the way you look, right there."

Willy smiled, squirming slightly. "And I love how this feels."

Reggie tugged off Willy's shoes and socks, then ran his fingers over his feet and up under his pants to his calves. Willy's legs shook in his hands, and he rubbed harder.

"Does it make me kinky because that feels so good?" Willy asked. "I heard that some people have fetishes about their feet, and...."

Reggie had to chuckle. "No. Having your feet rubbed doesn't make you kinky." He leaned over him, sliding his hands up Willy's legs and over his shirt to his collar. "I knew guys who liked to have guys fuck them with their toes. Now, that's kinky. I even met a guy once who loved it when he lay naked and multiple men pleasured him using just their feet. That's kinky."

"So I'm ordinary," Willy teased, and Reggie rolled his eyes.

"You, sweetheart, are anything but ordinary." Reggie grinned and pulled Willy's shirt up and over his head, baring his chest. He tickled around a nipple as Willy quivered on the bed. "Every guy has things he likes and places that turn him on. I found some of them last time, but...." Reggie flicked the hard bud with his tongue.

"Reggie...," Willy whined, and Reggie could tell he was still deciding if that really turned him on, or hurt because of the overwhelming sensation.

"Just go with it. Listen to your body and let it tell you what it wants." Reggie licked downward, across Willy's fluttering belly, swirling his tongue around his belly button. He couldn't get enough of him, salty sweetness reminiscent of the taffy from the seashore, only tastier, more addicting. "What does it tell you?"

Willy swallowed, and his mouth fell open, his eyes glassing over. "I want… I need…," he gasped, and Reggie tugged open Willy's belt and then his pants, parting the denim before pulling it downward. He pulled them off, dropping the fabric to the floor. Willy now lay on the bed nearly naked, his cock straining at the confines of his white briefs.

"What do you want?" Reggie inhaled, the room filling with the delicious scent of arousal and man. Willy was young, and Reggie had wondered if he was too young, but he definitely knew his own mind. The fire behind Willy's eyes proved that.

"I want you to make love to me. I need to know how you feel." Willy met Reggie's gaze with one as strong as steel. "You once told me that things were so good between us because we were making love. Well, I want to be sure. I want to know that you love me, because I know I love you." He sat up, tugged Reggie downward, and captured his lips.

Reggie was supposed to be the experienced partner in this relationship, but Willy was a fast learner, and he pulled Reggie into his orbit with ease. "How can you be so sure?" Reggie had to ask.

Willy slid back. "You're saying you don't feel anything for me?" He crossed his arms over his chest, glaring at Reggie. "Because if that's what you're trying to get me to believe for some weird reason, you're a liar."

"I am?" Reggie raised his eyebrows. "You see right through me."

"Of course I do. You, Sheriff, are an open book to me. You try to come off as a big badass, the powerful sheriff, but you're really just a great big bowl of mush. At least when you look at me." Dammit. Reggie tried to harden his gaze, and Willy laughed at him. "See? You can try, but I know you for who you are. You're a sensitive, caring man who's willing to put your own happiness aside for others." He rolled his eyes dramatically, and for a few seconds,

Willy looked so much younger. "Not many people are willing to do that for someone else." He unwound his arms and slid a hand behind Reggie's neck, leaving a trail of warmth in his wake. "I promise I won't tell anyone."

Reggie chuckled. "You better not, because this—" He looked down at both of them. "—is going to bring on a load of God knows what, and we're both going to need all the strength we can get."

"So there is an us?" Willy asked.

Reggie pounced, capturing Willy's lips as he wound his arms around him, holding tight. "You better believe it. I'll fight the very hounds of hell if it means keeping you safe and in my arms. The town, your father, and everyone else be damned. That is, if you'll have me." Reggie's stomach clenched and he held his breath.

"Have you? I wanted you that first night, and dammit, you made me wait so long. Of course I'll have you." Willy tugged open Reggie's shirt, buttons flying in every direction.

"That was a uniform shirt." Reggie looked down at what was left of it.

"Did I destroy police property? Are you going to have to lock me up and throw away the key?" Willy had a weird sense of humor. He giggled as he held out his hands. "Put the cuffs on me and take me in." He fell back on the bed.

Reggie shrugged off his shirt, and Willy's giggles died away. Reggie watched his throat work, swallowing hard, as he closed the distance between them to capture Willy's lips, pressing him back onto the bed. Reggie's control snapped. He delved deeply into Willy's mouth, taking what Willy gave and giving it back to him. He managed to slither out of his pants, groaning softly when Willy lightly bit his lower lip, adding roughness, earnestness, even desperation. Willy clutched him close, fingers digging into Reggie's back as he devoured as much of Willy as he possibly could.

He worked the last of Willy's clothes off, then removed the last of his own. "You are stunning. Have I ever told you that?"

"Once or twice," Willy said with a smile. "But I like hearing it." His eyes darkened, and Reggie closed the distance between them once again. Willy wound his legs around Reggie's waist and groaned as Reggie cupped his smooth butt in his hands. Few things were more exciting than Willy as he put himself in Reggie's hands.

Reggie liked being in control; it made him feel safe and secure. But there was nothing like the sounds Willy made when he was turned on, soft whimpers and moans that grew louder when Reggie worried that spot at the base of his neck or tweaked a nipple until he could hardly breathe. And when Reggie slid his lips down him, taking all of Willy's slender, long cock into his mouth... no song was ever as sweet or stirring.

"I want it all," Willy said, gripping the bedding. "All-the-way sex."

Reggie stopped. "Are you sure?" God, just the thought of being buried inside Willy's tight heat had his cock leaping for joy, but he didn't want to rush.

"Yes!" Willy cupped Reggie's cheeks. "Please. I want to feel you from the inside."

Reggie's breath hitched. He fumbled with the drawer of the bedside table, dropping the first condom on the floor and rummaging for another. He found the lube and then finally got his fingers around another foil packet, leaving the drawer where it was because he'd probably slam it shut with enough force to knock the lamp to the floor. It had been a long time since Reggie had been a virgin, but he felt like one tonight. His palms were sweaty, and his hands shook a little as he opened the lube, spilling more than he meant to on his fingers.

"I want to make this really good for you. If it hurts at all, just tell me and I'll stop right away." He teased Willy's opening, slowly sinking a finger into him. Willy grew still, and Reggie bit his lower lip until Willy gasped and groaned.

"Oh God." He clamped down on Reggie's finger, shivering a little.

Reggie took his time, listening to every breath, studying each moan and shake, watching as Willy arched his back, keening softly.

"I'm ready, please God, I'm ready." Willy drew him down into a kiss, deepening it quickly. "Don't make me beg. I will if I have to."

"I don't want to rush," Reggie said as his leg shook. He'd been ready for a while, his cock pointing to the ceiling, each of Willy's cries sending a wave of desire racing through him. With shaking hands Reggie reached for the condom, rolled it down his length, and slicked himself well. He knelt between Willy's legs, locking their gazes together, and slowly entered him.

Reggie's chest ached, in the best way possible, as the trust and love that shone in Willy's eyes nearly overwhelmed his senses when combined with Willy's heat surrounding him. He had to go carefully, even though every fiber of instinct pushed him forward. He had to take it slow. This was for Willy, to make sure he was happy. Reggie's own words echoed in his head about Willy being with someone who would make his first time special. At that time, in the parking lot of the club, he had never dreamed that weeks later, he'd be the one Willy trusted to take care with his first time.

"What are you doing?" Willy asked, pulling Reggie out of his thoughts. "Don't stop."

"I was just thinking about you." Reggie grinned and kissed Willy, holding still inside him, letting him adjust, and catching his own breath. "Something I've been doing a lot lately."

"Yeah. Me too. I think about you all the time." Willy groaned softly as Reggie began moving once again. This time his eyes rolled back and he gasped. "Damn...."

"I know." Reggie moved slowly, rolling his hips and making sure he kept pace with Willy's breathing. "You're driving me out of my mind."

"Me? You're the one with the rolly hips and the dick that keeps touching me in places I didn't know existed. Holy crap, you're making me see stars." Willy clung to him, and Reggie placed his hand in the center of Willy's chest.

"I know this is new, but I want you to look at me, feel me." Reggie took Willy's hand, placing it on his chest. "I can feel you. It's like you're part of me."

"I know." Willy held still as Reggie closed the distance between their lips. "I wish we could stay like this forever. When I'm with you, no one can touch me and I feel strong."

"You are strong. You proved that today." Reggie blinked back the moisture that filled his eyes. "I want you to stay with me. I want to look after you and have you look after me. I know it's awfully soon and we have a lot more we need to learn about each other, but that's what I want." He rolled his hips. "I want to sleep with you at night and wake up next to you. I want so many damn things, but I can't seem to think of what they are right now." He smiled and kissed Willy hard, driving them both toward the pillows. He'd tried using words to express what he felt and wasn't sure if he'd been successful, so he let his body do the talking, and if Willy's moans and whimpers were any indication, his message was getting through loud and clear.

"I love you, Willy," Reggie whispered as he reached the limits of what he could take. He was determined that Willy reach his pleasure first and held off by the skin of his teeth.

Willy groaned loudly, his body stilling, and then Willy's euphoria as he tumbled into release yanked away the last of Reggie's control and he careened into his own powerful orgasm.

Pink clouds carried him away, floating blissfully for a few seconds. As awareness returned, Reggie smiled, his joy increasing. Willy grinned up at him, his eyes half-lidded, looking debauched and so completely beautiful that it took Reggie's breath away. No words came to mind; this was too big for mere words. He was completely in love with Willy Thomas.

Reggie blinked to make sure this wasn't some sort of dream. Thankfully it was real, and he slowly climbed off the bed, took care of things, and returned with a cloth. Reggie lovingly cleaned Willy up, tossed the cloth and towel back into the bathroom, and climbed into bed.

"What do we do now?" Willy whispered.

"Sleep." Reggie wound his arms around Willy's waist.

"I mean, about my dad, the people in town, everything?" Willy rolled away from him. "I think I really messed up."

Reggie tugged him closer. "We take things one step at a time. Don't worry about your dad or the people in town, or anything else. Your dad will be who he is, and so will the good folks of Sierra

Pines. The important thing is that you chose to be who you are. That you don't want to live a lie… and I can't tell you how happy that makes me."

"Why?" That question was back. Reggie was quickly coming to believe that the day Willy stopped asking would be the day he died, and that was perfectly fine with him.

"Because you're here with me." Reggie kissed Willy's shoulder. "You did all that and then you called me." He held him tighter. "I'm in love with you. It's that simple. And I meant what I said. I will protect and care for you, and I'll move heaven and earth to make you happy, because you've made me happy."

"But how did I do that?"

Reggie closed his eyes, searching for an answer. Only one came to him. "I had these rules about how I was supposed to live my life. Be the sheriff here in Sierra Pines, and be a gay man everywhere else. But that pretty much sucked. I wasn't myself and I wasn't happy. You made me happy, and you are here with me." God, he wasn't even sure if he could explain it. Reggie knew he'd made a poor job of it. "Just relax and try to get some sleep. I know there will be repercussions and everything else on the horizon." But for right now, Reggie had what he truly wanted, and he wasn't going to let go if he could help it.

"But I have to ask, what if they fire you?" Willy bit his lower lip, and Reggie did his best to kiss the nerves away.

"Then I'll get another job, and I'll just have to hope that you'll come along with me." That was the only answer he had that didn't break his heart into a million pieces.

CHAPTER 11

GETTING OUT of bed after spending the night with Reggie had been nearly impossible. Reggie had to go in to the station, and Willy needed to go to the store for work. What Willy really would have liked would have been to hole up at Reggie's for a few days and hide from everything and everyone.

"Good morning," Mr. Webster said as Willy met him at the back door to open up. "Is everything okay?"

Willy shrugged. "I took your advice. I know you were right, but I was honest with my father and now I have no idea what's going to happen. He isn't going to be happy, that's for sure."

"Where did you stay?" Bless Mr. Webster for his concern. He unlocked the door, and Willy followed him inside.

"With Reggie." Willy closed the door and locked it from the inside. "I wasn't sure where to go. My friend Tony is in town, but he's staying with his family, and I knew I could count on Reggie."

Mr. Webster smiled. "That's because he cares for you, and you for him. Part of building a relationship is having someone to rely on. So what is it that's bothering you, besides your father?"

"It hasn't been that long. I met Reggie a few weeks ago, and now I came out to my dad and everyone in town is going to know. People will be talking about me, and who knows what's going to happen? Reggie is great, but what if he realizes I'm just some kid and he meets someone better and…?" Willy forced his mouth closed because he was rambling like an idiot. "I need to take a chill pill and stop everything from running in circles."

"Did you talk to Reggie?" Mr. Webster asked as he turned on the lights.

Willy opened the office door and paused before going in. "I don't know what to say." After last night and all the amazing things

144

Reggie had told him, he didn't want to ask a bunch of questions that made it seem like he had doubts.

Mr. Webster chuckled. "You kids. Everything is a big production and so full of angst and worry. Just tell him how you feel. I doubt a man like that is going to be upset or afraid. In fact, my guess is that he'll answer your questions as best he can." He passed Willy and sat in one of the office chairs. "What if he feels the exact same thing? Everything isn't going to be perfect for you or for him. There's a lot going on with his work, your work, and all the family drama."

Willy sat down, his leg bouncing. "I love him and I'm still scared."

"If you weren't, I'd be worried. My advice is to talk to him and take things one step at a time."

"What about my dad?" Willy said as someone knocked on the back door. Willy jumped up and went to open it. "What are you doing here?" he asked Reggie, who was a sight in his full sheriff's uniform.

"I wanted to bring you a key to the house." He set it in Willy's hand, and Willy nodded, looking at the small piece of brass.

"Thank you." Willy wasn't sure what else to say. "Ummm...." He stepped back, and Reggie came inside.

"We can talk about anything you want to, but I wanted you to know that you have a place to stay and that you can come and go as you need to." Reggie checked his watch. "I only have about five minutes before I have to be at city hall for a meeting. But don't worry, okay?" He hugged Willy, cradling him in his arms. "Just relax and try not to worry. Things will work out as long as you want them to."

Willy nodded. "I do. That's what scares me. Stuff doesn't work out very well for me."

Reggie smiled. "Then maybe things are about to change." He didn't move, just holding him for a minute, and some of Willy's inherent nervousness slipped away. "Text me if anything happens." Reggie released him and moved away. "I have to go." He took Willy's hand, teased his palm with his fingers, and leaned closer. "I meant what I said last night."

"I know. I love you too." Saying the words made Willy feel so much better. "I have to get things together so we can open."

Reggie nodded. "I know you're nervous, but remember who you are and what you did. That took guts."

"Amen," Mr. Webster said from the office, and Willy grinned.

"I'll see you tonight." Willy took a deep breath, letting go of a little more of the nervousness. Reggie was in this right alongside him. He wasn't alone. He had friends and people who cared, even if his family turned away, which he fully expected to happen.

Reggie hugged him again and then left. Willy closed the door and returned to the office to prep cash for the registers.

"You're smiling," Mr. Webster teased, clapping him on the shoulder. "Remember that feeling when things get a little tough and you'll be just fine." He left the office, and Willy finished the opening procedures and got the registers ready. Mr. Webster completed the rest of the tasks and opened the store as Willy got to work.

He spent his morning with his numbers and computer programs, getting everything up to date. Mr. Webster brought in some sandwiches, and Willy ate at his desk, then spent the afternoon working on the sales floor, building a display of snacks in preparation for the weekend's games.

"Willy."

He knew that voice. "Hey, Mom," he said quietly, turning around and catching Ezekiel as he ran at him.

"I missed you," Ezekiel said.

"I missed you too." Willy returned his hug and set him down once more. "How are…?" He wasn't even sure what to say.

"Sweetheart, go pick out one candy bar for yourself and one for Ruthie." She sent Ezekiel off and turned to him. "You worried me when you left. Are you safe?"

"Yes, Mom. I'm fine. I have a place to stay with Sheriff Barnett. He's a really good man, and he cares about me." Willy hugged her tightly. "I couldn't stay there with Dad. I hope you know that."

She hugged him back fiercely. "I do. Your father doesn't like to admit it, but he has a temper and…." She clutched him even tighter. "I let him get away with some of the things he did because I was scared of him too."

"I'm not scared of him anymore, and I won't let him dictate the rest of my life. I'm out on my own now and that's how it's going to stay. I have a job, and maybe I'll get an apartment. Reggie gave me a key to his house, and I really like it there with him. He's a special man." Willy stepped back as the bell on the front door rang with a customer. This was a place of business, after all.

"I hope so." She held his hand. "Your father and I have been talking a lot, and things have to change. We both went into a holding pattern after Isaac died, and I don't think either of us broke out of it. We've been grieving for years and it's time we stopped. I want to, but I don't know if your father has figured out how he can do that." She reached into her purse and pulled out a tissue to dab her eyes.

"You have to, for Ruthie and Ezekiel. They deserve a life that's more than regimen and going to hell. They need fun and laughter. We all do." Willy squeezed her hand. "And, Mom, they deserve the chance to be who they are. Whether Dad agrees with it or not. So do I, and that's what is going to happen." He sighed. "Please tell Dad that if he wants to talk, I'll listen, but he's going to have to come to me. I will not seek him out." He hugged her again and waved at the boxes. "I need to get back to work."

"Please come to dinner," she said. "I want to be able to see you."

Willy nearly nodded. "I'll think about it. But is that invitation only for me or for Reggie too?" His mom didn't answer. "Think about it." He turned as Ezekiel came running up the aisle with two bags of M&M's in his hands, grinning. That was a real treat for him, and he was excited.

"Be good."

"Will you let me read you a story tonight?" Ezekiel asked.

"Not tonight, but soon, I promise." Willy turned to his mother, and she nodded. He knew this was hurting her and that jabbed at him. "I can't go back to the way things were. I just can't." He hoped she understood. "He can be so overbearing, and I have to go my own way.

147

No matter what he thinks." Then he went back to work, realizing just how much he had to lose.

WILLY WAS scheduled to leave the store at five, but Mr. Webster was super busy, so he stayed on, watching the sales floor and helping customers.

"Oh my God, are you okay?" Tony asked quietly as he approached. "You finally did it."

Willy gasped, and Tony rolled his eyes.

"I knew. Please. Not that it matters to me, but your dad had to have gone through the roof. Reverend Gabriel's son, gay." Tony put his hand over his mouth dramatically and then fanned himself. "He's held himself and the entire family up as this paragon of virtue and perfection for so long that his ears have to be ringing about now." He looked around. "How are you holding up?"

Willy smiled. He loved Tony's energy. "I'm okay. I was kinda prepared for this to happen, so when I told him, I just left. I didn't stick around to see what he'd do or how he'd react." He leaned closer. "I even managed to turn the tables on him a little and make the conversation about him and the kind of father he's been." Willy held up his hand, and Tony high-fived it. "I told him I wanted my dad back… and I do." He steadied himself. "What have you heard?"

Tony glanced around again. "Well, let's see. So far there isn't a consensus. But I did hear that the sheriff has corrupted you." He faked a gasp. Sometimes Willy wondered if Tony shouldn't be the gay one. "I heard that from a friend of my mom, and I told her that was a bunch of crap. Gay or straight is who you are, not something you choose. She argued with me, and I told her to get over it and that you deserved to be treated fairly and not be the subject of gossip. Mom said the same thing, and that ended that topic."

"Great. I suppose that's as good as I can expect."

"Well, actually, I don't think most people really care. So you're gay. There will be a few busybodies who talk and all that, but a lot of them just have to have something to talk about. These people have known you since you were a toddler. You've always been nice, treated your brother and sister with care."

"They don't hate me?" Willy asked as two ladies came inside. One looked at him and turned away. The other walked straight over to him with her mouth open, but seemed to think better of it and patted him lightly on the shoulder as she passed.

"See? People will think what they want, but fuck 'em. Most people are cool and pretty awesome." Tony flashed a grin. "I'm here for a few more days and then I have to go back, but if you want to go…." He turned his attention out on the street. "Damn," he whispered under his breath as Reggie strode by. "He's enough to turn me on to men." Tony slapped him on the back.

"But what if they go after him?" Willy voiced his deep-seated concern.

"That man can take care of himself, and I'm willing to bet half the gossips in town are upset about the fact that he's gay and, therefore, out of the marriage pool, because I bet some ovaries went into overdrive every time he passed."

Willy had to stop himself from laughing. "You're bad."

"I know. Maybe I should be a screenwriter rather than an actor. Maybe I could break into the movies that way." Tony smirked, and Willy rolled his eyes.

"Don't quit your day job." They shared a laugh as Mr. Webster came out of the back. He waved, and Willy got his things to get ready to go.

"Is Reggie working?" Tony asked. "We could have dinner if you want."

"I'd have to text him, but he probably is. There have been some troubles he's been working on." He sent the message, but Reggie responded that he would be late. Willy told him he was going to dinner with a friend and to meet them at the diner if he was able to.

They left through the back, and Willy drove to the diner and parked in the lot behind it. He was a little nervous about how people might react, but no one really seemed to pay them much attention. Sue greeted them, and they took a table.

"How are you doing, honey?" Cindy asked when she came to take their order. "Your dad could be all holier-than-thou just a little too much. So you stick to your guns." She straightened up and took their drink orders.

"See? Lots of people don't care, and even more will defend you." Tony flashed a smile and flipped through the menu. "I'm going to get a salad. My dad has been cooking out and filling me so full of fried chicken and frozen meals that I need to watch my waist or no one is going to hire me." He told Cindy what he wanted, and Willy ordered a BLT with a side of onion rings.

"Hey," Willy said as Reggie approached and slid into the booth next to him. "You remember Tony."

"Good to see you again." They shook hands.

"How did it go at city hall?" Willy asked.

Reggie smirked. "They tried to give me some grief, but there isn't anything they can do. Mayor Fullerton was supportive and said that it was completely immaterial. The man was what counted, not the person he fell in love with." Reggie grinned and bumped his shoulder. "He's really changed his tune." Reggie waved Cindy over and gave her his order. "I only have a little while and then I'm going to need to go."

"Is something happening?" Tony asked.

"I believe it's possible, so I need to be watchful." Reggie's gaze met Willy's. "When you get to the house, be sure to lock all the doors behind you." It was a weird thing for Reggie to tell him. People didn't always lock their doors here, so something truly must be happening.

"Of course I will."

"Willy tells me that you're an actor," Reggie said as Cindy brought Tony's salad and then returned with the rest of the food.

"I'm trying to be. It's hard to break in and get noticed. Everyone comes to LA with huge dreams to somehow break into the movies. I thought it would be so easy to do." Tony shrugged. "I learned pretty quickly that it's a lot of hard work. But I'm giving it my best and I still have hope. I've done some good work, and I have a callback next week. I actually made it through the first round of cattle-call auditions for this part on a sitcom. When I came in, I did the role as pretty queeny, even though the guy is supposed to be straight, and my agent said they loved it. So who knows." He grinned as he took a bite of salad. "How about you? Why law enforcement?"

"It was something I always wanted to do. Mom and Dad had different ideas, but this makes me happy and I'm good at it." Reggie took big bites of his burger, practically swallowing the thing whole.

"Slow down. No one is going to take it from you." It was pretty obvious that Reggie was wound up and anxious. Willy ate more slowly and slid out when Reggie was done.

"I have to get back." Reggie squeezed his hand. "I'll see you tonight, and remember what I told you." He left more money than was necessary on the table and hurried out.

"You are one lucky guy," Tony observed.

Willy leaned on the table. "I am, I agree. But why do you draw that conclusion?"

"He's so intense. The last woman I dated who was like that… well, let's just say that girl was freaky good and she blew my mind. She was up for anything, even some stuff that I would never have thought of. Holy cow, that was an awesome six weeks."

"You broke it off with her?" Willy asked.

"No, her husband came home. I didn't know she was married, but suddenly… well, you know. It's hell being the boy toy." Tony groaned for two seconds and then split into a grin. "It was fun while it lasted."

"You're awful."

"Hey, I was the one being used. Apparently she thought me a lot of fun." He shrugged. "Like I'm going to complain. It happened, it was fun, and now it's over."

"Do you date at all? Like, seriously?" Willy asked.

"I have, and there's a woman I really like. I've seen her out a few times and she's a lot of fun. I've talked to her a bit, but I don't know if she's interested. She works as a model and is really busy. I'd like to be able to spend some time with her and get to know her, but I've gotten this reputation, sort of, and I think she's a little scared that

I'm only after her for sex or for who she is… or something." Tony set down his fork. "I just want to take her out."

"Then ask her. But be clear that you want to get to know her. Ask her to dinner, or better yet, offer to cook for her. I swear that's what got Reggie's attention. I cooked for him, and it worked."

"You know I don't cook," Tony groused. "I can heat stuff up just fine, but cooking… I burn water." He made a face, and Willy rolled his eyes.

"It's about patience and taking your time. I can give you some easy recipes if that's what you want to do. I could even talk you through the cooking." Willy was excited for his friend. He finished his sandwich and bit an onion ring, then passed one to Tony when he saw him eyeing them ravenously. "If you get the date, I'll have your back with the food."

Willy turned toward one of the other tables when a commotion broke out. It settled down once more, and he looked back at Tony. "Are people watching me?"

"Maybe a little," Tony said. "But they've pretty much returned to their own lives. When they see that you're like everyone else and are just as boring and uninteresting as you always were, they'll forget all about it." He smirked, and Willy smacked his arm.

"That's pretty mean, even if it is true. I have to be about the most boring person on earth." Again, why would Reggie be interested in him long-term? Eventually he was going to find out that there was very little special about him and then that would be it.

"Stop it. I was teasing. I've known you a long time, and you are not boring. So stop worrying." Tony scowled at him. "Just relax. That man thinks you hung the moon. It's clear as day every time he looks at you." He leaned over the table. "I'd give a lot to have someone look at me like that, so don't think twice about it. Be happy and enjoy being in love." He finished his salad and ate the onion ring, then snagged one more from Willy's plate before they were all gone.

"Do you need me to take you anywhere?"

"No. I can walk back to where I parked my car." Tony paid for his food, and Willy chucked in his share, making sure Cindy got a good tip, and then they left the diner. Willy said goodbye to Tony, sharing a quick hug. Tony walked down the sidewalk toward the other end of town, and Willy went the opposite way.

In his car, he pulled out and turned onto Sierra Drive. He turned left, heading out toward Reggie's house. A white van passed him going the other way. Willy recognized it instantly. He stopped, made a turn, drove around the block, and then turned back on Sierra going the other way. The van was stopped at the only light in town. Willy grabbed his phone and called Reggie, but it went to voicemail.

"Reggie, I see the white van. I'm behind it on Sierra, and it's heading north out of town. Please call me. I'm going to try to follow them for a little while."

He hung up and drove slowly, not getting too close, merely taking the highway out of town. He kept the van in view around curves and caught sight of it on the hills. It pulled into the rest area, so Willy stopped on the side of the road. He called Reggie again, and the call went to voicemail again. He sent a text and waited a few minutes before pulling into the rest area. He parked next to the van and got out to use the restroom. This time when walking beside the van, he listened carefully. Whispers reached his ears, but he didn't dare spend too much time in case he was being watched. He stepped away and went into the bathroom, which was deserted. He used the facilities, washed his hands, and got ready to leave.

This was completely stupid, and Reggie was going to give him major hell once he saw him. Willy was sure of that as he dried his hands and left the restroom, intending to go right back to his car. Men stood near the van, leaning against the hood. Willy purposely paid them no attention as he walked to his old car. He pulled open the driver's door and was about to get inside when someone grabbed him from behind, yanking him away from the car.

"Settle down or I'll break your fucking neck," the man growled, pulling Willy back hard enough he almost fell.

"What do we do with him?" another man asked.

"Open the back door," the man holding him demanded.

Before Willy could react, he was tossed inside, hitting his head on the floor of the van. His ears rang as the door slammed shut, and then it was quiet. His thinking muddled and his head aching, he tried not to pass out. Willy was afraid to open his eyes, but he had to see where he was.

Three sets of fearful eyes met his, all of them of Asian descent. The van smelled acrid, like terror in the close quarters. They said nothing and all backed away, looking at each other and pressing against the walls. Willy reached into his pocket to pull out his phone. The screen was cracked, and when he tried to unlock it, nothing happened. When the engine started, he knew he was in deep trouble.

"You stay where you are and don't try anything, or we'll dump you where no one will ever find you except the wolves and bears."

The window closed to the cab, and the van started to move.

CHAPTER 12

REGGIE SWORE as he listened to the message, pressing the accelerator and flipping on his lights. He called back but got no response. He zoomed through the light in town as he spoke into the radio. "All units available, north on Sierra." He described Willy's car and then called directly into the switchboard. "Marie, get me through to the Reverend Gabriel."

"Yes, sir," she answered, and after a few seconds, the line rang and connected.

"Reverend, this is the sheriff and this is an official call. Has anyone in the family seen Willy in the last little while?" Reggie had to try to make sure he wasn't back in town. It was a long shot, but he had to try.

"No. What's happened?" Reverend Gabriel seemed truly concerned.

"I'm not sure. He left me a message about following a van that he'd seen before." Reggie continued driving, speaking through the car's phone connection, as his anxiety went supernova in seconds.

"Approaching the rest area," Jasper said, answering his call.

"Hold on." Reggie switched to the radio. "Check out the area. Report anything you find." His stomach clenched, and he switched back to the phone as he flew through the light, heading north as fast as he dared.

"I'm doing my best. Make calls to be sure he isn't with his friends." Reggie rattled off his direct number. "Call if you find out anything. I'm trying to find him right now."

Reverend Gabriel agreed, and Reggie hung up and switched back to the radio.

"Willy's car is at the rest area. It's empty, and the rest area is deserted. No sign of anyone."

"Shit. Willy said he was following a white van headed north. We need to find it. They haven't passed me. Take the back way to the county line, and we'll set up a roadblock. I'm approaching the rest area now and will continue on the highway."

"On it, Sheriff," Jasper acknowledged.

Reggie flew past as Jasper got ready to pull out of the rest area. Every second counted, and Reggie hoped to hell they weren't too far ahead. He went as fast as he dared, lights and sirens blazing, the car trembling as he took curves and damn near went airborne over bumps. Still, he didn't dare slow down. He'd just found Willy, and he'd be damned if he was going to lose him. Reggie would trail them to the state line and beyond if necessary.

He caught sight of a flash of white approaching a curve about five miles later. "Jasper, where are you?"

"On Highlands, going as fast as I can. Maybe eight miles from the county line."

"I have them in sight. Suspect van heading north. I am in pursuit," Reggie called, concentrating on his driving. All Reggie had to do was stay with them. They weren't going to get away from him.

"Will intercept," Jasper answered.

The van slowed and made a turn on two wheels, nearly overturning. Reggie skidded, back wheels sliding around the corner before digging in, and he shot after them. He radioed his new position and pushed onward, keeping in constant contact as he continued pursuit.

The driver's actions were becoming more erratic. Reggie could almost feel their anxiety, and that scared him even more. If he was hell-bent on getting away, the driver was going to make a mistake that could cost everyone in the van their lives.

"I'm on River Road, heading your direction," Sam added.

"Excellent. We're approaching that intersection, maybe ninety seconds. Get there!" Reggie gripped the wheel as tightly as he could, slowing up a little. If Willy was in that van, Reggie hoped he was safe and that he got to him in time. He also hoped that giving the van some space would ease the tension on the driver and he'd be more careful.

It wasn't likely, but he had to try to keep everyone in the van as safe as possible.

"ETA sixty seconds," Sam said, and Reggie breathed deeply as the van nearly took a curve too fast.

His phone rang and he answered it. "Sheriff," he said, heart racing faster and faster, his reflexes growing sharper by the second as his heart rate continued to climb.

"Reverend Gabriel here. No one has seen Willy." He sounded distraught. "I called everyone I can think of. He was at dinner with his friend Tony, who seems to be the last person to have seen him." He sighed into the phone.

"We located his abandoned car at the rest area. We are in pursuit. I will call when I know anything. Thank you for checking. I will do everything I can to get him back." Reggie wasn't even sure if Willy was in the white van, but it was the only lead he had and he was going to pursue it with everything in him.

"What can I do?" Reverend Gabriel asked. "He's my son and...."

Reggie hesitated as the van rocked hard from side to side over rough road, and he avoided the same spot as best he could. "Pray, please. I think we'll all need it. I'll call you as soon as I know anything more. Thank you for your help." He ended the call and sped up, running on the edge of safety. If they lost the van, Willy and whoever else might be in there would have very little chance of survival.

He ended up slowing down as they approached the intersection. Sam's car spanned the lanes and there was no place for the van to go. Reggie braked and pulled to a stop, with Jasper gliding up behind him a few seconds later. Clearly the rookie had been paying attention and adjusted his actions. Reggie flipped on his speaker. "Get out of the van and lie down flat on the pavement."

The passenger door opened and a man got out. He turned and fired at Reggie's car, the mountains amplifying the blast. The windshield spidered but remained in one piece, except for a hole and the one in Reggie's seat. He got down, brandishing his gun, ready for action. Fire returned from behind him, and then the scene grew quiet.

He opened the driver's door and slowly got out, using the door as a shield, keeping low.

"You all right, Sheriff? One suspect down," Jasper said.

Reggie brandished his gun as the driver's side door opened and a man got out. "Put the gun down and lie flat on the road. You have two seconds," Reggie bellowed.

The man dropped his gun and fell to the ground, arms above his head. "I give up," he said, voice muffled. "Don't shoot."

"Cover me," Reggie told Jasper as he hurried up, kicked the gun away, checked out the van cab interior, and then cuffed the man on the ground, leaving him there for now. "What about the other one?" Reggie asked Jasper.

"Sam has him," Jasper called as Reggie finished securing the man on the ground.

"Get control of the firearm and log it into evidence." He wasn't going to let him up until that was done.

Jasper put the gun in a bag and secured it. Then and only then did Reggie stand and step away.

"Get him to your car and call an ambulance for the other guy." Reggie stood as Jasper took charge of the suspect, and went to the back of the van. He held his gun at the ready and pulled open the door.

The scent was the first thing that assaulted his senses. He turned away to breathe fresh air as the acrid scent of unwashed bodies and a lack of basic hygiene hit him like a steamroller. Four sets of eyes peered at him, three near panic and one he was so relieved to see that Reggie's knees nearly buckled from under him.

"Jasper," he called loudly as he began helping people out of the filthy van. The women didn't appear to speak English, and Reggie helped them out gently before guiding Willy into his arms. "Are you hurt?" Damn he wanted to strip him down right here just so he could check him over and make these assholes pay for every scrape or bruise.

"No. I'm okay. Just banged around. But please help them. I don't think they've had food or water in a while."

This was the most amazing man. God knew what he'd been through and he was worried about the others.

"I have some water in the trunk." Reggie unlocked the trunk of his car, and Willy hurried over, grabbed bottles, and handed them out to each of the women. He also found Reggie's stash of snacks and handed those out as well. The women were truly hungry, stuffing the food in their mouths and gulping the water. Reggie wanted to tell them to slow down and not eat too quickly, but he didn't have the words.

"What do we do now?" Willy asked gently.

Sam joined them. "I hope it's okay, but I contacted the state police. They're on their way. I explained the situation, and they were sending an Asian-language specialist. Hopefully he can help them."

The women had finished eating, and they sat by the side of the road, talking softly among themselves. Reggie didn't understand a word, but he was fully aware of how worried they were from their tone.

A siren reached his ears, getting louder, and an ambulance joined them. They took care of the injured prisoner, strapped him in, and took off. Jasper followed with the other prisoner in the back. A second ambulance arrived, and the EMTs checked over the three women, pronouncing them malnourished but otherwise healthy. Sam stayed with the women while Reggie arranged for a hotel room for them. The least he could do was help them clean up and sleep for the night.

Sam seemed especially gentle with them, and they seemed to respond to him, so Reggie thought he'd made a good choice. Finally, once the suspects were gone, as well as the victims, he turned to Willy. "What were you thinking, following them? You took a decade off my life." He pulled Willy into a tight hug. "Don't you ever do that to me again. I don't think my heart will be able to take it." He clung to Willy as just how close he'd come to losing him hit like a bomb.

"I called you, but you didn't answer, and I only thought to see where they were going so you could take over. I was leaving the rest area when they grabbed me. I think they were taking me north. The women don't speak English, but they said a few words. One of them was 'Canada.'" He stopped. "Next time take my call, okay?" Willy slapped him on the shoulder. "I was only trying to help."

"Help send me to an early grave. Yeah, I can see that...." Reggie sighed and stood stock-still for a long time and then released Willy, motioning him to the car. They got inside, and he drove back to town, handing Willy his phone. "You need to call your family and let them know you're okay."

Willy groaned. "You called them?"

"Your father checked with everyone he could find to make sure you weren't still in town. He saved us a lot of useless searching and allowed us to catch up with them much faster."

Willy stared at the phone and then entered the numbers. He glared at Reggie, but there was nothing to be done about it now.

"Father," Willie said. "Yes, I'm fine. Reggie caught up to them and saved me." His voice broke. "I'm really okay. They traffic in people. They were using the rest area as a stop-off. I think they sometimes pick up people there and deliver them. I heard the drivers talking." Tears ran down Willy's cheeks, and Reggie was about to pull over to try to comfort him. "They were going to kill me. I know that. They needed to get me away from town. I could hear them talking. They figured they'd get me a couple hours away and then kill me and drop me somewhere in the woods. I'd never be found, and that would be that. But Reggie saved me." Willy broke down. "I'm okay, Dad, really," he said through his tears. "I was really scared, but I knew Reggie would come for me. He's the best, and he said he'd always protect me." Willy wiped his eyes, and Reggie reached over to take Willy's hand.

Reggie wanted to comfort him, but he also had to get back to the station. There was a lot of work ahead, and God knew what surprises were in store. He had a feeling that these arrests were only the beginning of this case.

"I really am, Dad. This is a lot to take in, but I saw the van and I called Reggie and followed it. I'd seen it before and, well...." He coughed and cleared his throat. "Reggie is the best kind of man. He's a lot like you used to be before Isaac died. ... I know, Dad, but you gotta try. I miss him too." Willy let go of Reggie's hand and wiped his eyes. "Is that what's really important? So Reggie is a man and I'm in love with him. How many texts are there about loving your neighbor? And let's not forget 'judge not….' Dad, you've been doing a lot of judging. Try being happy for a change. I know that's what I'm going to try." He gulped and lowered the phone, pressing the button to end the call.

"Is it okay?" Reggie was very concerned, but the conversation had sounded positive and Willy had actually referred to his father as dad, which was something Reggie hadn't heard him do very often.

"I think so, yeah. He isn't as sure about stuff as he always was, and maybe that's about as good as things are going to get." Willy handed back Reggie's phone and turned to look out the window, wiping his eyes once again. "Thank you for saving me."

Reggie slowed down as he reached the edge of town and pulled into the station. "I'll do whatever it takes to keep you happy and safe. Period. If that means chasing some asshole all the way to the gates of hell, I'll do it." He parked and they got out of the car. "I'm going to get a statement, and I need to treat you as a witness. I'm going to assign Jasper to work with you because I can't do it. I need to maintain some professional distance."

"I get that," Willy agreed and followed him inside.

All hell had broken loose in the station.

Marie and the deputies were yelling. Jasper and Shawn stood chest to chest, seconds from fighting. Sam was trying to separate them, but that didn't seem to be working. Marie was in the corner, actively trying to get away.

"What is going on?" Reggie bellowed at the top of his lungs, using all the power in his voice. They all came to a standstill.

"One of our suspects recognized Shawn here," Jasper said without turning away from him. "He needs to surrender his weapon and stand down now."

"All right. Jasper, stand down." Reggie turned to Sam. "Did you hear anything?"

Sam nodded. "The suspect who wasn't shot tried to go after Shawn. He actually asked him where he was and why he hadn't warned them. He called Shawn every name in the book."

Reggie already had his hand on his weapon. "That's enough. Shawn, step into my office, now." He watched Shawn's hands as he followed him. "Sam, take charge of the suspect and check with emergency services to make sure our wounded suspect is in a secure hospital ward. Jasper, you interview witnesses and take statements. Let me know when the state police folks arrive." He closed the door, keeping Shawn in his sights.

"Don't tell me you're going to believe some criminal?" Shawn said indignantly.

"Right now, I need to be cautious. You will surrender your gun and badge. As of right now, you are suspended." Reggie got no satisfaction from that. He had never trusted Shawn and thought he might be up to something, but human trafficking? Making money on the misery and degradation of others? If it was true, he was going to wring his neck.

"You can't be serious." Shawn stood, legs apart, trying to intimidate. Reggie was having none of it. "You've hated me since the first day you arrived, and you've had it in for me. And now some scum says something and you use it as an excuse to fire me?" He set his gun on the desk, and Reggie took it and locked it away, instantly feeling better.

"Actually, it's you who hated me. You liked the way things were. You ran things under the old sheriff, and you basically had the run of the town and could set up your own little business ventures. I have a witness who can place your personal vehicle at the rest area. I suspect it was a meeting with your business partners. I didn't have any proof then, but I've been watching." Reggie stood. "I will get to the bottom of this, fairly quickly. If you are involved, so help me, I'll roast you on a spit." He opened the door. "You are to stay at your desk and not to leave the building. If you do, I will issue a warrant for your arrest so fast, it will make your head spin." He glared at Shawn and watched as he left the office and sat at his desk, arms folded over his chest.

Reggie stopped by the switchboard and asked Marie to keep an eye on Shawn. "If he tries to leave, call me and you can arrest him."

"Really?" she asked with a wide smile.

"You betcha." Reggie returned her smile and looked over the station. Jasper and Willy sat at a desk, talking softly. He went in search of Sam and found him in the interview room. Reggie went to watch through the one-way mirror. The suspect sweated, pulling at his collar, then ran his hands through his scraggly brown hair. He seemed to be talking and Reggie didn't want to interrupt, so he waited until Sam stood, left the room, and joined him.

"Holy cow," Sam said quietly. "I put plenty of pressure on him and he cracked like an egg. The guy isn't too bright, and I don't think he knows all that much about how things worked. But he was to stop at the rest area to let the women use the bathroom. He says he did that, like the Good Samaritan he is, and then he was supposed to wait because someone was to bring two more girls. Then he was to drive them north to Seattle, where they had jobs waiting for them." He groaned, and Reggie knew exactly what kind of work they'd be doing. The women most likely had no idea and thought they'd be working in a factory or maybe as domestics. But they were pretty under the dirt and awful clothes… so their work was more likely to be prostitution.

"Did he say who he was supposed to meet?" Reggie asked, watching the suspect fidget. He hadn't expected Sam to get so much information from their suspect. It seemed he might have hidden skills, which was awesome.

"No. He didn't have a name, only that he'd know him by a code word: 'thistle.' He did know that if he got into any trouble, he was to call a deputy who was in the know. He most definitely recognized Shawn in the station room, and I asked specifically about him. He said he'd seen him on multiple occasions, and while he didn't know Shawn's name, he identified him, as well as his car." Sam showed Reggie his notes.

"So even if we get Shawn, there's someone else?" Reggie groaned. "And I know who it is, I think, and this is going to get really ugly."

There was very little doubt about that. "Talk to him some more. Get as much as you can about this other man and the specifics about when he met Shawn. I want to nail him to the wall and see if our colleague will turn on his cohorts."

"You got it," Sam said.

"Call if you get stuck," Reggie told him and left Sam to his task. He returned to the station and sat down across from Shawn, staring at him without looking away.

"What?" Shawn grunted.

"It seems the hole is opening up beneath you." Reggie flashed a smile. "I have one suspect singing like a canary, and I'm on my way to the hospital to talk to the other. I bet he'll sing louder and longer to save his miserable skin." He stayed where he was, loving the way Shawn's upper lip twitched. Then he got up and checked in with Jasper, who had finished with Willy.

"I'll type up the report and have Willy sign it."

"Good. When it's done, let me know and I'll take Willy to his car on my way out to the hospital." Reggie was now pretty sure he was short a man and thought about who he might get to replace Shawn. He pulled his attention back to the present and what he had to get done. Thankfully the state police arrived with their interpreter. He set him up with the three women and spoke with the lead officer in his office.

"Jack Penner," Jack said, shaking Reggie's hand after his own introduction.

"Thanks for coming," Reggie said, sitting at his desk.

"You busted a trafficking ring. Good work. We've been after some of these guys for a while." Jack seemed extremely pleased.

"I have a complication. One of my deputies is involved. I have enough evidence to arrest him, but the witness is one of the drivers. I need something more in order to get the charges to stick. I'm heading over to the hospital to speak with our other suspect, and then we'll go up the ladder."

Jack grinned. "You know who it is?"

Dang, Reggie would have thought it was Christmas day.

"Yes. But I'm not letting on. Let him stew a while and see just how much progress we're making. Shawn is getting more frightened by the second. He doesn't have his phone and I shut off the one at his desk, so all he can do is sit and worry. It's a beautiful thing. Let him see his world coming to pieces a little at a time all around him."

Jack chuckled. "That's diabolically brilliant. I'll have one of my officers sit with him and we'll increase the pressure. So once we're ready to talk to him, he'll spill his guts just to try to save his own skin."

"That's my plan. I need him to roll over on his boss like a dog for a treat. He's already sweating bullets. We'll see what our ladies have to say, and then we need to do what we can to help them."

"Already on it. You go talk to your suspect, and we'll hold things down here."

"I appreciate the help. I'm a deputy shy, for obvious reasons." Reggie called Sam into the office and made introductions. "Work with Jack to get him whatever he needs. I'm going to take Willy to get his car and then go to the hospital." Reggie stood. "Call me if you need anything."

He had one long night ahead of him, and he needed to get started.

THE LIGHTS were dim when Reggie finally got to the house. The television flashed through the front window, so he knew Willy was there. He parked in the garage, went inside, and found Willy asleep on the sofa.

"Hey, sweetheart. You should have gone to bed." Reggie turned off the television and scooped Willy into his arms. Willy curled into him, barely stirring as Reggie carried him to bed.

"I'm sorry. I tried to stay awake," Willy mumbled. "Is everything okay?"

"Yes. Shawn is in a cell and I'll talk to him in the morning. Both suspects fingered him as involved in the ring. He can sit in jail overnight. I'm too tired to deal with him." Reggie set Willy on the bed, then pulled back the covers. Willy tugged off the shorts and T-shirt he was wearing and snuggled down under the covers.

"What about the women?"

"They're in a hotel, and we've made sure they have enough to eat and drink. The state police are working with them to get them back to their families. Most likely they'll be deported. They had been brought over illegally and apparently were lured with the promise of a good life and job. The state police will be able to see to it they aren't harmed." Reggie yawned. "The rest will wait until morning." He turned out the light and went to the bathroom to brush his teeth and clean up before joining Willy under the covers.

Willy was already asleep, thank goodness. Reggie had been worried he might be really upset, but he seemed to have taken what happened fairly well. Granted, it would probably catch up with him later. He curled next to Willy, holding him close, saying a silent prayer to the powers that be for delivering him safely. That was the most important thing for him. Willy was safe, and Reggie had been able to find the rotten apple in his department. The rest he could deal with in time.

"Reggie?" Willy asked, rolling over. "Are you sure this is all going to be okay?"

Reggie held Willy tighter. "I really hope so. Jack is working to help root out the rest of the organization, and as soon as I have proof on the leaders, we'll go after them as well. It's not going to be long before we'll be able to follow the trail to the people we need to." Reggie kissed him gently. "Just go to sleep and try to put it behind you. I'm here and you're safe."

WILLY WOKE with a start, pulling Reggie out of a sound sleep.

"It's all right."

"Someone's here." Willy pushed back the covers, got out of bed, and pulled on his thin robe.

A tentative knock sounded, and Reggie rolled over, groaning at the time. Figuring whoever was at the door at this hour wanted him,

Reggie yanked on his pants, got out of bed, and hurried through the house to the front door, with Willy behind him.

Reggie opened it, surprised to find the Reverend Gabriel on his front porch. He looked at Willy and then back to him, prepared to shift into guard mode if necessary. "Can I help you?"

"I'm sorry about the hour, but I haven't slept all night and I need to see my son."

There was no pushiness or even the hint of harshness in his voice. Reggie detected a ton of parental worry, and he stepped back, letting him inside. Turning to Willy, he put an arm around his waist in an effort to ease the worry that filled his eyes.

"You scared your mother and me half to death. Are you okay? Did you get hurt at all?"

Willy shook his head slowly, staying where he was. "I'm fine, Dad. I got a little banged up in the back of the van, but Reggie found me very quickly and they didn't get a real chance to hurt me." He approached but stayed behind Reggie, taking his arm. Reggie inched closer. "I'm sorry you and Mom were worried, but everything is okay, as I told you yesterday."

Reggie stayed between them as Reverend Gabriel stepped closer.

"I know things have been… difficult between us. But I want something different. I want something better." He wrung his hands. "I don't know what to do. My beliefs tell me one thing, and yet my son… it's very difficult." He sighed and grew quiet.

"You were always so sure of yourself, that what you believe is right. But, Dad, that's wrong. Your beliefs are just that—an opinion, nothing more. Yes, you feel strongly, but so do I, and I won't acquiesce to what you think any longer. I have to live my own life. Reggie helped show me that." Willy held his arm tighter. "Maybe we can come to an understanding. We might be able to get along. But that requires that you accept that I am the man I am."

Reggie could feel the strength building inside Willy. It had always been there, but now it rose to the surface and stayed there.

"Reverend, I love your son." Reggie turned to Willy, sharing a smile. "This isn't some passing infatuation. He's strong and smart, gentle, and an incredible man."

"Reggie," Willy said, blushing adorably, in Reggie's opinion. But that display of affection only made Reverend Gabriel more nervous, shifting his weight slightly from foot to foot.

"I was hoping to convince you to come home and be part of the family again. To...."

"To do things the way you want and be under your thumb?" Willy shook his head. "I'm not coming back to that house of grief and pain again. I won't live under your thumb anymore. This is my life, and I'll find my own path." Willy stepped around and up to his father.

"You're going to live here?" Reverend Gabriel asked.

"I don't know. I have a job now, and I'm looking at places to live. I may not have my entire life planned out, but I'm on my own, living my life, and it's going to stay that way. People in town may talk about me or look at me funny, but I don't care. They'll get over it as soon as there's something or someone else to talk about. The thing is, do you want to be part of my life or not?" He put his hands on his hips, and Reggie wished he could see Willy's eyes right then. He could only imagine the steel in them. "I don't believe the same things you do. Can you live with that?"

Reggie touched Willy's shoulder just to remind him that he was here for him. This had to be one of the hardest, most difficult things anyone could do, disagreeing and stepping away from a parent.

"I guess I'll have to learn," Reverend Gabriel said. "You are still my son and I still love you." His lower lip trembled. "I don't know how I can come to understand the choices you've made or—"

"Dad, being gay isn't a choice. It's part of who I am. You and Mom didn't do something to make me this way. It's just how I was born." Willy stepped back until he touched Reggie. "I could deny who I am, but that would only lead to a life of misery." He reached out and took one of his father's hands. "You always said that God didn't make mistakes, we did. Well, then I am who I am and I'm not a mistake.

If you want a relationship with me, you need to accept that." Willy released his hand.

Reverend Gabriel stood still, blinking. Reggie had seen that world-rocking look a few times before. The man looked shell-shocked and out of his depth. Part of the bedrock he'd thought he'd built his life on had been changed to sand, and he didn't know what to do about it. "I—"

"I got some really good advice from a friend the other day. Think about what you really want, Dad. Are your beliefs so central to you and who you are that they're worth the loss of your son?" Willy waited a few seconds, but Reverend Gabriel made no indication of his feelings. Then Willy turned and walked back down the hall toward the bedroom, the click of a door closing ringing through the house.

Reverend Gabriel nodded and turned. "I'm sorry for bothering you so early." He left the house, and Reggie closed the front door and then returned to their room.

"Sweetheart," Reggie said as he went inside. Willy sat on the edge of the bed, raising his head as Reggie came inside. "I'm so sorry…," Reggie said quietly.

Willy shook his head once and wiped his eyes. "No. There's nothing to be sorry for. My father… Dad… is who he is, and I can't change that. Only he can, and he doesn't do change well at all. So…." He shrugged. "At least we were able to talk, and that's about as much as I can hope for." He stood, reaching for the knob. "I should get dressed. Maybe I can find a place to live."

The thought of Willy leaving sent a stab of pain racing through Reggie's heart. "Stay here. You can have the guest room if that's what you want." Reggie tugged Willy closer. "I mean, you don't have to stay here in this room with me. Sharing my bed isn't a condition of—" God, now he was as nervous as a long-tailed cat in a room full of rocking chairs.

"Do you want me to stay? Really?" A smile rose on Willy's lips like the dawn, slowly and brightly.

Reggie cleared his throat. "Dammit, yes, I want you to stay. And if we're talking about what I want, then I want this side of the bed to be yours and that one to be mine for as long as you'll have me. I want you to smile when you see me in the drugstore, and I want to see that look in your eyes whenever I'm in my uniform." Reggie grinned and wiped his own eyes.

"But it's only been a few weeks, and—"

"Then keep your things in the guest room if that will make you feel better. We don't have to rush. As long as you're safe and sound and I can hold you—" Reggie tugged Willy into his arms. "—then we can face anything, including the town gossips, your father, and God knows what else will come our way." He smiled as Willy nodded and drew closer.

"But isn't that a lot?" Willy asked tentatively.

Reggie shook his head. "No. It's a small price to pay… for you." He closed the distance between them. There was still plenty to do, but he had what was important, and the rest he could take care of… later….

He pressed Willy back onto the bed. Definitely later.

Epilogue

INSTRUMENTAL CHRISTMAS music played in the background as Willy worked to fill the candy display. This time of year, the store was always busy, which was wonderful. Willy had designed and installed the window displays, as well as a lot of the other decorations for the store. It was very festive, and Mr. Webster was pleased mainly because he didn't have to do it.

It turned out that after all the years in business, Mr. Webster was a bit of a Scrooge. "I just want this season to be over," he said softly as he approached. "Every year it's the same thing. They want the one item I didn't order enough of, and they complain about it for days." He rolled his eyes. "The family is always so excited, and I get home completely exhausted from the long hours."

"Why don't you ask them to work? They're old enough to help. Maybe have them earn money for the holidays," Willy offered. "I can keep them busy."

Mr. Webster chuckled. "I bet you can. Heck, you could run this store without any help from me." He patted Willy on the shoulder and handed him an envelope. "It's your Christmas bonus and a notice of a raise. You deserve it."

Willy opened the envelope, blinking at the amount. "This is too much."

"No, it's not," Mr. Webster said, patting him on the shoulder again and hurrying to the back of the store where a customer was asking for him.

Willy blinked at the five-hundred-dollar check. He put it in his pocket and went back to work, finishing up his display. He took the empty boxes away and got the last of the Christmas items from the back. There were still two weeks until Christmas, and it looked like they were going to have a sellout of the holiday items, which was awesome. Everyone in Sierra Pines seemed to be in the holiday spirit.

"Willy!"

Willy stowed the cart just outside the stockroom as Ezekiel barreled into him. He hugged his brother, lifting him into his arms.

"I did really good. See?" He showed Willy a paper from school with a star and a smiley face on it. "I get lots of those."

"That's awesome," Willy said. "Are you here with Mom?"

Ezekiel shook his head, pointing as Willy's father approached, with Reggie not far behind him. Now that was a strange sight.

"Dad?" Willy asked. He hadn't seen his father very much over the past few months, and when he had, he was cool and rather aloof. He hadn't said anything bad or hurtful—distant was probably the best description Willy could come up with.

"Reverend," Reggie said as he joined Willy. "I came to take you to lunch, but it looks like you already have company."

"Ezekiel, why don't you go see if you can find something for your sister for Christmas?" his father offered, and Ezekiel hurried down the candy aisle. Goodness knew what he would pick out. "Willy, Reggie," his dad began, "I…." He fidgeted. "We are having a family gathering Christmas Eve and wanted to invite both of you."

Willy turned to Reggie as a shot of excitement jolted through his veins. "Did Mom put you up to this?"

His dad hesitated. "No. It's time I put aside some of my pride and stubbornness." The hurt in his dad's eyes told Willy he was being truthful. "You're my son and I'm your dad, and it's time I started acting like it again. At least I'm going to try." He looked to both of them. "Please come." He turned away, following behind Ezekiel, and a childish squeal of delight rang through the store as his father scooped Ezekiel into his arms, both of them laughing.

"Can we go?" Willy swore he wasn't going to cry, but dammit, he was so close.

"Of course we can. I'll call my parents and let them know that we'll need to adjust our plans a little. They were having their get-together for Christmas dinner, so it will be fine." Reggie put his arm around him, and Willy instantly felt as though the spinning world had calmed once again.

"Thank you. This is the first sign that...." It was hard for him to say.

"I know, sweetheart," Reggie said gently. "Why don't you go tell Mr. Webster that you're leaving and get your coat so I can take you to lunch? There's a lot I want to tell you."

"Give me a minute," Willy said, then hurried to the office to get his coat. He told Mr. Webster he was going to lunch and slipped on his coat. He waved to Rose at the register as he left, and she waved back.

Wisps of snow fell around them as they walked to the diner. "I thought you were in Sacramento and weren't going to be back until tomorrow."

The human trafficking case had quickly gotten much larger than their small town. The tendrils of the organization had reached as far away as Los Angeles and San Diego. It seemed that Reggie had been able to pull enough threads of the organization and Jack followed them back to their origins. Dozens of people had been arrested.

"Shawn pleaded guilty, and he fingered James Calder, who also pleaded guilty. They will be spending a lot of time behind bars, but their cooperation is going to send a lot of worse people away as well. So that part of the case is over. The state approved the money for an additional deputy to aid in making sure this type of thing doesn't get a start in our area again."

"So you have to hire two deputies?"

"Just one more. Jack says he wants to join the force here. He likes the area and has been looking to find a place where he can settle down. He'll take Shawn's spot as my lead deputy, and I'll do a search to fill the new position. Jack will start just after Christmas. I should have filled the position a while ago, but I wanted to make sure anyone I hired would fit in here."

"You think Jack will?" Willy asked, pulling open the door of the diner.

"Yeah. He told me his boyfriend left him a year ago and he's been looking to get away and start somewhere new." Reggie winked, and Willy chuckled. "Both Sam and Jasper worked well with him and they already know him, so it should be a pretty easy integration." They found a seat, and Willy took off his coat, waiting for Reggie to do the same before sitting down. "The entire town needs a chance to digest what happened."

"Yeah, but considering no one really liked Shawn, and James Calder was a self-important jerk, I think they'll get over it, especially now that the trial is over and the story can fade from the news and stuff." Willy picked up a menu and glanced over it before setting it down again. He knew it by heart and ordered his favorite chicken salad. "I'm glad you're back."

"Me too. It's supposed to storm tonight. They're calling for eight to ten inches of snow. I was trying to get back before it started." Reggie ran his fingers over Willy's before pulling his hand back. Just about everyone knew they were a couple. Most people went about their business, though a few tried to cause trouble, but they didn't get very far. Basically he and Reggie were careful in public.

"It's good to have you home," Willy whispered softly. "The house always seems so empty." Their bed certainly did.

AFTER LUNCH, Willy went back to work and then drove home. Reggie's house had quickly come to feel like home, and Willy associated Reggie with that feeling, so when he was gone, the place never seemed to warm up, no matter how much he tried to heat it. It just felt empty when Reggie wasn't there.

Willy pulled into the garage, went inside, and got things together to make dinner. Reggie came in a little while later, turning on all the Christmas lights to make the house seem more festive. Sometimes Reggie was just a big kid.

"What are we having for dinner?"

"I have a couple of steaks and some mashed potatoes. I also got fresh carrots at the market. Is that okay?" Willy asked as Reggie walked around the kitchen work area, took Willy by the hand, and led him to the sofa.

"I know it's early, but I have your Christmas present. I tried to wait until the day, but it hasn't worked out."

"Reggie, it's too early. Just wrap it up and put it under the tree. I'll wait until then." He wasn't Ruthie, who peeked at everything under the tree well before the holiday. His mother always hid her presents.

"I don't think I can do that." Reggie stood. "Wait here." He hurried away, returned with a large box, and set it on the floor in front of him.

Willy huffed and opened it. A large black puppy tried to climb out of the box, and Willy reached for it, hugging it immediately to his body. The puppy licked Willy's chin, squirming and wiggling like crazy.

"His name's Bear and he's a black lab. The people who originally took him couldn't keep him. I had hoped to find someone to hold him until Christmas, but I figured it was better that he got settled in his new home."

"Reggie," Willy said softly. "This is…." He wiped his eyes as Reggie sat down next to him.

Reggie leaned closer, sliding an arm around him. "This way you won't be alone when I have to go away. And just so you know, my parents have already invited their new grandpuppy for Christmas."

"Thank you. I always wanted a dog…." Willy pressed in for a kiss. "This is perfect. I love you so much." He kissed Reggie deeper until the puppy squirmed and whined. Willy set him down, and he wandered through the room, exploring and smelling. "Does this mean I won't have a present on Christmas day?" Willy laughed as Reggie pushed him back onto the cushions.

REGGIE KISSED away the question, knowing that the ring rested at the bottom of his sock drawer, already wrapped, just waiting for Christmas morning.

ANDREW GREY grew up in western Michigan with a father who loved to tell stories and a mother who loved to read them. Since then he has lived all over the country and traveled throughout the world. He has a master's degree from the University of Wisconsin-Milwaukee and now works full-time on his writing. Andrew received the RWA Centennial Award in 2017. His hobbies include collecting antiques, gardening, and leaving his dirty dishes anywhere but in the sink (particularly when writing). He considers himself blessed with an accepting family, fantastic friends, and the world's most supportive and loving husband. Andrew currently lives in beautiful historic Carlisle, Pennsylvania.

Email: andrewgrey@comcast.net
Website: www.andrewgreybooks.com

BURIED
PASSIONS

ANDREW
GREY

"Sweet and spicy,
poignant and hopeful,
Buried Passions is
a pleasure!"
~Karen Rose,
NYT Bestselling Author

When Broadway actor Jonah receives word that his uncle has passed away and named him the heir to a property in Carlisle, Pennsylvania, Jonah's plan is to settle the estate as quickly as possible and return to his life in New York City. Much to Jonah's surprise, the inheritance includes the Ashford Cemetery—and its hunky groundskeeper, recent Bosnian immigrant Luka Pavelka.

Jonah soon discovers Luka is more than easy on the eyes. He sees into Jonah's heart like no man ever before, and his job at the cemetery is all he has. If Jonah sells, Luka is left with nothing. Luka is there for Jonah when Jonah needs someone most, and there's no denying the chemistry and connection between them. But Jonah has a successful career back in New York. Now he must decide if it's still the life he wants….

www.dreamspinnerpress.com

FIRE AND *Flint*

ANDREW GREY

A Carlisle Deputies Novel

Jordan Erichsohn suspects something is rotten about his boss, Judge Crawford. Unfortunately he has nowhere to turn and doubts anyone will believe his claims—least of all the handsome deputy, Pierre Ravelle, who has been assigned to protect the judge after he received threatening letters. The judge has a long reach, and if he finds out Jordan's turned on him, he might impede Jordan adopting his son, Jeremiah.

When Jordan can no longer stay silent, he gathers his courage and tells Pierre what he knows. To his surprise and relief, Pierre believes him, and Jordan finds an ally… and maybe more. Pierre vows to do what it takes to protect Jordan and Jeremiah and see justice done. He's willing to fight for the man he's growing to love and the family he's starting to think of as his own. But Crawford is a powerful and dangerous enemy, and he's not above ripping apart everything Jordan and Pierre are trying to build in order to save himself….

www.dreamspinnerpress.com

SETTING the HOOK

ANDREW GREY

Love's Charter: Book One

It could be the catch of a lifetime.

William Westmoreland escapes his unfulfilling Rhode Island existence by traveling to Florida twice a year and chartering Mike Jansen's fishing boat to take him out on the Gulf. The crystal-blue water and tropical scenery isn't the only view William enjoys, but he's never made his move. A vacation romance just isn't on his horizon.

Mike started his Apalachicola charter fishing service as a way to care for his daughter and mother, putting their safety and security ahead of the needs of his own heart. Denying his attraction becomes harder with each of William's visits.

William and Mike's latest fishing excursion starts with a beautiful day, but a hurricane's erratic course changes everything, stranding William. As the wind and rain rage outside, the passion the two men have been trying to resist for years crashes over them. In the storm's wake, it leaves both men yearning to prolong what they have found. But real life pulls William back to his obligations. Can they find a way to reduce the distance between them and discover a place where their souls can meet? The journey will require rough sailing, but the bright future at the end might be worth the choppy seas.

www.dreamspinnerpress.com

TAMING THE BEAST

ANDREW GREY

The suspicious death of Dante Bartholomew's wife changed him, especially in the eyes of the residents of St. Giles. They no longer see a successful businessman… only a monster they believe was involved. Dante's horrific reputation eclipses the truth to the point that he sees no choice but to isolate himself and his heart.

The plan backfires when he meets counselor Beau Clarity and the children he works with. Beau and the kids see beyond the beastly reputation to the beautiful soul inside Dante, and Dante's cold heart begins to thaw as they slip past his defenses. The warmth and hope Beau brings to Dante's life help him see his entire existence—his trials and sorrows—in a brighter light.

But Dante's secrets could rip happiness from their grasp… especially since someone isn't above hurting those Dante has grown to love in order to bring him down.

www.dreamspinnerpress.com

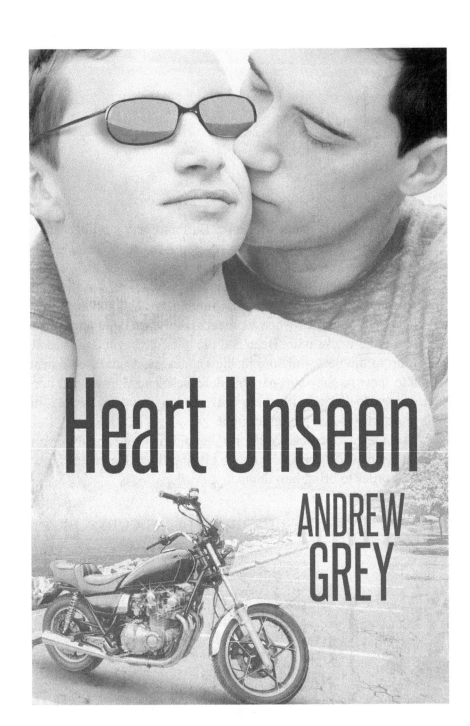

Heart Unseen

ANDREW GREY

A Hearts Entwined Novel

As a stunningly attractive man and the owner of a successful chain of auto repair garages, Trevor is used to attention, adoration, and getting what he wants. What he wants tends to be passionate, no-strings-attached flings with men he meets in clubs. He doesn't expect anything different when he sets his sights on James. Imagine his surprise when the charm that normally brings men to their knees fails to impress. Trevor will need to drop the routine and connect with James on a meaningful level. He starts by offering to take James home instead of James riding home with his intoxicated friend.

For James, losing his sight at a young age meant limited opportunities for social interaction. Spending most of his time working at a school for the blind has left him unfamiliar with Trevor's world, but James has fought hard for his independence, and he knows what he wants. Right now, that means stepping outside his comfort zone and into Trevor's heart.

Trevor is also open to exploring real love and commitment for a change, but before he can be the man James needs him to be, he'll have to deal with the pain of his past.

www.dreamspinnerpress.com

Heart Unheard

ANDREW GREY

A Hearts Entwined Novel

The attraction between Brent Berkheimer and Scott Spearman peels the wallpaper, but Brent is Scott's boss, and they're both too professional to go beyond flirting. Their priorities realign after Scott is badly injured in an accident that costs him his hearing, and Brent realizes what is truly important… he wants Scott.

Scott pushes Brent away at first, fearing a new romance will just add to his problems, but perhaps he will find unexpected strength and solace in Brent's support as he struggles to communicate with the world in a new way.

Just as they decide the chance of a happy future together is worth the risk, Scott and Brent discover darker challenges in their way—including evidence that the "accident" Scott suffered may not have been so accidental.

www.dreamspinnerpress.com